Danica stared him down.

Let him get angry. She didn't care.

Her finger thrust against his rock-hard chest. "I waited for you." Her voice shook. She squared her shoulders. "When I took the first pregnancy test, I was alone. I've been alone every step of the way, except for my family. My girls are Bergmanns, and that's all they know. You showing up on my doorstep does not change the fact they don't have a father. They never did, and they're fine—better than fine."

Mouth open, Reid didn't say a word. From deep in the back of his throat, his voice emerged. "They're mine."

"No. You gave up that right when you decided it was easier just to vanish than tell me what was happening. I'm not talking to you about them."

Unable to deal with his self-inflicted wounds any longer, she marched past him and into the office. Slamming the door felt better than it should.

A seventh-generation Texan, **Jolene Navarro** fills her life with family, faith and life's beautiful messiness. She knows that as much as the world changes, people stay the same: vow-keepers and heartbreakers. Jolene married a vow-keeper who shows her holding hands never gets old. When not writing, Jolene teaches art to inner-city teens and hangs out with her own four almost-grown kids. Find Jolene on Facebook or her blog, jolenenavarrowriter.com.

Books by Jolene Navarro

Love Inspired

Lone Star Legacy

Texas Daddy
The Texan's Twins

Lone Star Holiday
Lone Star Hero
A Texas Christmas Wish
The Soldier's Surprise Family

Love Inspired Historical

Lone Star Bride

The Texan's Twins

Jolene Navarro

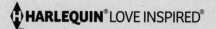

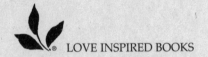

PLEASE RECYCLE · THIS PRODUCT IS RECYCLABLE

Recycling programs
for this product may
not exist in your area.

LOVE INSPIRED BOOKS

ISBN-13: 978-1-335-50870-6

The Texan's Twins

www.Harlequin.com

Printed in U.S.A.

He will turn again, He will have compassion upon us; He will subdue our iniquities; and thou wilt cast all their sins into the depths of the sea.
—*Micah* 7:19

This book is dedicated to the tribe of women that I get the blessing of calling my aunts. Kathy, Dollye, Nellie, Molly, Jan, Melody and in memory of Trish. Thank you for being role models and inspiration throughout my entire life.

I can't go without acknowledging the people that have made the dream of being a writer my real life.

The brainteam: Alexandra Sokoloff's 2016 group at West Texas Writer's Academy. Also Sasha, Storm and Damon. And a special thanks to Jeannie Lyons for all her help. And Matt Sherley for the insight into the background information of Reid's arrest.

To my agent, Pam Hopkins, for believing in me even when I completely doubt myself.

To my editor, Emily Rodmell. Thank you for working so hard to make my stories the best they can be.

Chapter One

The numbers blurred on the computer screen as the reality of Danica's financial situation became clear. The bank statement bore the proof that her dream of a thriving animal sanctuary was morphing into a nightmare. She rubbed her eyes and opened the grant proposal file.

Linda Edward had trusted her to take care of the fur babies. Danica's father thought it was a waste of time and money, but it wasn't only her dream in jeopardy. The animals depended on the facility. There were a couple of big cats and a crippled bear that had nowhere else to go.

She leaned back and sighed. Was she fighting so hard just to prove her father wrong? He had always been right before. Glancing above her desk, she took the time to count her blessings.

Most days, the montage of family pictures and her daughters' artwork inspired her. Including one photo with her and her mother bottle-feeding an injured fawn. It had been taken the week before her mother's accident. Danica had been the same age her twins were now when she lost her mother.

Her sisters reassured her their mom would be one hundred percent on board with the sanctuary. Nikki, her oldest sister, told her to ignore her father's grumbling. It was just his way of dealing with anxiety. With her history, he had a good reason to worry.

Scanning the happy memories and big life events, she realized one was missing. The only photo from her wedding. It was hidden away in her room, deep in her closet. She'd thought about burning it, but one day her twins might have questions.

Her daughters. Her fingertips brushed the rhinestone clusters along the edge of the frame the girls had made. They had their father's beautiful eyes. As much as Reid's abandonment had almost destroyed her, he'd also given her the greatest gift. Her five-year-old twins inspired her to be a fighter.

Leaning back, she pulled a folder from the cabinet behind her. Enough musing— she had a future to figure out. The past was the past.

Danica needed a plan to save the animals. Otherwise, the wildlife rescue would be forced to close its doors, and she'd lose the land. The spiral of death swirled on the outdated computer. Waiting, she swiveled the old office chair to the right. The large window faced the east.

From here, she could see a couple of ponies playing with a miniature donkey. They'd been rescued from a roadside carnival, and now the trio romped in the sun.

Finally, the file opened. Before she started, a vehicle crunched the gravel in the front drive. Praying it was the exciting news James had hinted about at church on Sunday, she made her way to the door. As the local parole officer, he often sent her workers that needed community hours. Free labor was always a win.

The old unmarked Uvalde County car came to a stop at her door. Hope surged through her veins. James Bolton was also on her board, and he knew she needed someone who could manage the unique diet plans and daily health issues of multiple species, along with transportation. It was hard to find trained and experienced people who were willing to work for free. If he had a parolee with that background, it would be a perfect fit for what she needed to complete the application.

Standing next to the patrol car, James

waved. "Hey, beautiful. I come bearing gifts. You can take me to the movies to show your gratitude." He wiggled his dark blond eyebrows.

She shook her head and grinned. The county officer was always flirting with her, but she never took him seriously. "James Bolton, you'd hate the movie I'd make you see." She glanced to the passenger's side of the car. He went around to open the back door, but the man stayed inside. With the partition between the seats, she couldn't make out much.

If he was a vet tech, she might run and hug him. On the edge of the step, she turned to James. "Please tell me your latest ward is certified in animal husbandry?"

"Yes, ma'am."

Everything inside her wanted to dance and sing. She lifted her face to the sun. *Thank You, God.*

A hand appeared on the top of the door, and in slow motion the man straightened.

His head stayed down, the cowboy hat blocking his face. He was over six feet tall and well built. Younger than she'd expected. He didn't move. She hoped he was all right.

The man just stood there for a while. He removed his cowboy hat and slowly raised his head. His eyes reached hers.

A rush of ice froze her blood in its place. There was no way. She could not be seeing the person she thought she was seeing. It didn't make sense. Rubbing her eyes, she looked again. His dark skin highlighted startling gray-green eyes that stared straight at her. The exact same eyes as her daughters'.

"Danica, this is my latest parolee, Reid McAllister. He comes with exceptional references and the experience you need. Reid, this is…"

James kept talking, but he no longer existed in her world. Reid McAllister stood in front of her. The man who had vowed to love her forever, before she knew how short forever was.

After a six-year vanishing act, her husband, the father of her twins, stood at the steps of her sanctuary.

Her heart stopped, and her knees went numb. To remain standing, she wrapped her fingers around the post. Her girls!

In a panic, her gaze darted around the area. The girls weren't here. They were safe with her sister. Forcing her attention back to James, she took a deep breath and tried to gain control of her brain.

That was a problem she always had around Reid. Crazy sounded fun and reasonable. But the impulsive, reckless girl she'd been was gone now. She needed sensible, rational thoughts.

No one knew she was foolish enough to elope and marry a man her father didn't even like, except the man standing in front of her. A parolee.

Reid in prison? She was going to lose her lunch.

Strong fingers gripped her elbow. Blinking, she focused on her friend. He was safe. James stepped closer. "Do you need to sit down? Are you sick? What's wrong?"

He led her to the large wooden bench by the front door. Looking over the uniformed shoulder, she found Reid. At some point, he had moved closer to her and now stood at the bottom of the steps, hands in his pockets.

His expression was as hard as the cold stone of the Texas Hill Country. This man wasn't her Reid.

Her Reid had always had a smile and a spark in his eyes for her. The gray-green of his irises struck her, but they looked flat and cold now. His black hair was cropped close to his skull. What had he done to end up in prison, and why hadn't he told her?

She rubbed her head. "It hurts."

"I'm going to get you some water and aspirin. Don't move." James disappeared through the front door.

Reid was as still as a snake trying to hide in the tall grass. He just stood there and stared at her, his full lips in a small snarl. Acting like a rescue animal that didn't trust anyone, even the ones trying to help. He had no right to be mad at her. She was the injured party here.

"Are you dating him?" Each word tight and low.

Anger jolted through her. Standing, she took a step forward, then stopped. "Six years without a word and…that's not any of your business."

There was a slight shift in his expression, but then the I-couldn't-care-less face was back in place. He shrugged. "Are we still married?"

"What?" Lowering her head into her hands, she dropped back onto the bench. She just couldn't process this. "I got one call from you, telling me our marriage was a mistake. That was it. No way to get ahold of you to make sure you were all right. You were just gone. I thought you had gone back to New Orleans."

Through a haze of confusion, she studied his face. His throat tightened, but there was no other change in his expression. "You show up at my door, asking me if we're still married. You can't be real."

She'd thought a new parolee had been an answer to a prayer. Was this some horrible joke?

Reid looked down the drive that had brought him here. "Baby, as soon as he comes back, I'll tell him I can't do it. He can take me back to the ranch."

"Which ranch?" Sweat slipped down her spine, causing her to shiver. His voice made her want to cry for everything he had taken from her. Baby. She used to love the way he called her baby with that accent.

That voice carried her back to the days she loved just sitting and listening to him talk. He had been twelve when Katrina sent his family to Houston. The rhythm and sounds of New Orleans still rolled off each syllable. She shook her head. It didn't change what he did. "Reid, I don't understand. Why are you here?"

"I took a job at Hausman Ranch. I'm a wrangler." The door opened, and Reid retreated. She needed to talk to him, to find out where he'd been. Why had he left her? Prison. Why had Reid been in prison? Questions bombarded her brain faster than she could process them.

Her nails cut into her palm. If she didn't know yesterday, she didn't need to know today. He was her past and needed to stay that way.

James sat next to her. "Here, take this."

She took the painkiller he offered and the mason jar of ice water. Long slow drinks of the cool water soothed her burning throat. She needed time. Her brain was overloaded. "Thank you." She cupped the large-mouth jar in both hands and studied the ice before risking a glance in Reid's direction.

He stood with his hands braced on the top of the car, head down. "Officer Bolton, can you take me back? She doesn't want a convict working at her place."

James shook his head. "I bring her parolees all the time." With narrowed eyes, James faced her again. "Plus, she needs someone with your skills. Danica, are you sure you're okay? Do you want me to call Jackie or your dad?"

"No!" Taking a deep breath, she willed her blood pressure to slow down. "I'm fine. I've been sitting all day working on the paperwork for the application. I didn't eat lunch. I must have gotten up too fast. Just dizzy."

James didn't look like he believed her. With one hand on her shoulder, he leaned closer. "Are you sure? You need to take better care of yourself."

She managed a smile. "Yes, I'm sure."

Reid turned. Leaving his profile for her to study. There was a harder edge to his jaw than she remembered. A scar that hadn't been there before cut next to his ear. Her stupid heart missed a beat. No, no, no.

With his back now leaning on the patrol car, he stared out across the five-hundred-acre sanctuary. He crossed his arms, causing his shirt to pull tight over his broad shoulders. He'd filled out, gotten stronger. *He's been in prison.*

"Reid was a pre-vet student from your old stomping ground over at A&M. In prison, there was a rodeo program, and he worked with large animals. He was able to finish an associate's degree in animal husbandry. You need him to get the funding, right?" James turned to Reid. "She's in a rough place, and the sanctuary needs the global certification to qualify for a grant that will give her the funds needed to keep the place running."

His gaze found her. "So, you're the veterinarian?" A line formed between Reid's eyes as he spoke.

"I didn't finish college. I had to come home my junior year." Let him think about that.

James kept talking as he stood. "No, she's

not the vet. Dr. Ortiz out of Uvalde serves as the vet. I sit on the Hill Country Wildlife Rescue Board. When I got your paperwork, it was a true gift from God. Thought I'd surprise her and get to play the hero. You know, save the day, keep the sanctuary open and all that." He laughed. "Actually get a date."

"James." She was not in the mood to deal with his jokes.

Reid's head jerked around, his sharp gaze penetrating. "Without my help, you might have to shut down?"

She hated to admit it, but yes. She needed Reid McAllister. Well, the animals needed him. She didn't want anything to do with him. With a nod, she got to her feet. "Yes." She had to wonder at God's timing.

Bobby, the groundskeeper, came from behind the building. Even though he was pushing seventy, his tall frame moved with well-earned confidence. He outworked any of the younger guys she had on the property. The sun weathered his face, digging deep creases into his skin. With his steel gray mustache, Danica liked to think of him as her own Sam Elliott.

The officer greeted him and shook his hand. "Reid, this is Robert Campbell. He lives here on the grounds and takes care of everything. Reid here has a degree in animal husbandry."

Bobby stepped forward and offered his hand. "You're one of Jimmy's parolees?"

Reid gave a stiff nod as he shook the older man's hand. "Yes, sir."

"What were you in for?" Bobby kept Reid's hand firmly in his. They stood eye to eye, both over six feet with the muscular frames of hardworking men.

"Transporting drugs across state lines." His stance and gaze stayed steady as he met Bobby's question head-on.

She pressed her hands against her rapid heartbeat. She needed to calm down. "Did you do it?" Her voice struggled to climb out of her throat. She couldn't imagine her

Reid doing anything like that. Maybe he'd been framed.

He pulled his hand from Bobby's and shrugged. "When someone offers you a couple thousand dollars to drive a car from one state to another, you know. Even if you don't ask and they don't tell. But I thought a short-cut to money was worth the risk."

"Sounds like there was a girl you wanted to impress." Bobby adjusted his cowboy hat. "It's always about a girl. I had a little run-in with the law myself when I was younger. It didn't pay off." He glanced at his watch. "Well, I got animals waiting for me." He nodded at Danica. "Remember, I'm just one click away if you need anything." Turning back to Reid, he pointed to his walkie-talkie. "I always have this, so if she needs me, I'm there. Nice meeting you." With the last word, he left.

James shifted his attention to Danica. "Are you feeling better? I could bring Reid back tomorrow."

If she wanted a fighting chance to keep the sanctuary running, she didn't have a choice. "I'm good. Whatever it was, I'm over it."

She was over loving her husband, too, so why did he have to show up now and throw her heart into an undertow? Pulling her denim jacket tighter over her chest, Danica peeked at Reid from the corner of her vision. She was stronger than some leftover love that had dug into the bottom of her heart. "I could take you on a tour if you still want to do your community service here."

He nodded. Grim would have been a happy description compared to the hard set of his jaw and eyes.

She was going to have to keep him away from her daughters and her family. What would he do if he found out he was a father? Would he even care?

Reid fell in behind Danica. Somehow, she was more beautiful than the last time he'd seen her. Of course, he hadn't known it would be the last time.

Easy money was never really easy. Reid had known better, but he'd thought a few days to make enough money to impress her father would set them on the right path. The few days had turned into six years, and he was pretty sure her family hated him now more than back then.

It was not the path God intended. But being young and impatient, he hadn't had enough faith to wait. Now the best thing that had ever happened to him was out of his reach.

Officer Bolton took a call and moved away from them. Danica stopped and glanced back at the officer.

Being this close to her was dangerous for his sanity. The sun was high over the hills, and a soft breeze played with her red curls, picking up golden highlights. A random strand crossed her face, and she tucked it away only to have it fall loose again.

Her hair always fascinated him. He'd called it red. She'd told him it was strawberry blond. From that day on, he'd loved strawberries.

She wore it shorter now. In college, it hung below her waist. Fisting his hands, Reid stuffed them in his back pockets to keep from touching her.

This was not how he'd imagined their first meeting, and he had spent hours daydreaming about it. Then again, prison wasn't in his plan on the day he had promised to love her forever.

She cut a hard glare at him. Caught staring, he suddenly found his worn boots fascinating. He had no right to be thinking of her or looking at her.

From the corner of his eye, he glanced at the porch. She scanned the area with short jerky movements. Taking a step closer to him, she twisted and lowered her head, trying to make eye contact with him. He gave in and stared right at her.

The connection didn't last long. Danica quickly looked away. "You've been in prison? I don't understand. Why are you here now? After all this time?" She bit her lip and straightened. Back stiff and arms crossed, she looked off to the surrounding hills.

Reid had always loved the way she showed her emotions around him, not afraid or ashamed. But now he could see her fighting back the tears, fighting to be stoic with each blink. Her bottom lip disappeared between her teeth. Instinct told him to hold her, to reassure her.

Stalling for time, he cleared his throat and prayed for the right words. Fully aware there weren't any. "Baby, I know sorry is not good enough for what I did to you, but it's all I have."

No explanation was good enough. He shrugged. "I didn't mean to show up on your doorstep unannounced this way. I didn't know he was bringing me to you." His throat was still dry, but he had so many words he needed to say to her. "He just told me a wild-life rescue program needed a vet tech."

When his mentor had showed him a list of jobs needing his skills, he couldn't believe there was a ranch close to her hometown. Wanting to see her so badly, he thought maybe it was God giving him an oppor-tunity to make it right. Now he realized it could have been his pride. "If me being here is a mistake, let me know and I'll leave."

An annoyed sound came from her beau-tiful lips. "What did you hope to achieve? I've moved on. You told me you had decided to go home. That our marriage was a mis-take and you wouldn't be back. One phone call and you left me without a way to get in touch. You just left." Her breathing was short and hard.

The numbness that encased his heart a couple of years ago slipped a bit, and he stood before her with fresh wounds. He rubbed his face and focused on the hills. He didn't have the strength to be near her and not want to be in her life. She had been his until he'd destroyed their future. He knew right then that without her forgiveness, he was still in prison.

"Danica, our marriage was a mistake. My family tradition is failure, prison and violence. I thought I had escaped, but it followed me. I'm not asking to be part of your life, but I'm here with the skills you need. Let me help until you get someone else." He clenched his jaw and looked over her shoulder at the building behind her. Chipped paint revealed years of neglect.

His own father had destroyed his beautiful Creole mother. Now the promises he'd made Danica lay shattered on the ground. To keep his hands out of trouble, he stuffed them in his pockets. His gaze was not as easy to control. Tall and lean, she was so much stronger than his mother.

At least he hadn't brought children into this mess.

Without a word, she stared at him. Guilt and shame were heavy burdens to carry. Lowering his head, he took deep breaths. In prison, he'd learned really quickly to avoid eye contact, and it was hard to change the habit.

Officer Bolton joined them. "Call just came across the radio. During a drug bust on the edge of the county, they got a surprise in the basement. They found a caged bear and an old black jaguar. The cat has a bad leg. There was talk of putting the animals down. I told them I was with you, and we could transport the animals here. I already called Dr. Ortiz to meet us there." He smiled at Reid. "Initiation by fire. It looks like you're jumping into the deep end today."

Reid looked at his wife. No, he couldn't think of her in those terms. It was too dangerous to get wrapped up in what could have been. Her hard glare felt like heat burning his skin, starting at his neck and traveling down.

Bolton slapped him on the back, causing him to jerk around. The officer laughed. "You go in the truck with Danica. She'll update you. I'll wait for you to gather your things, and you can follow me." With a big smile, he headed to his patrol car. "Welcome to the world of rescue."

"Come on, Mr. McAllister." She didn't wait for him. "I need to get the supplies. Have you moved large sedated animals before?"

He followed. "A few times, Mrs. McAllister."

She stopped in front of him, and he bumped into her back. His hands went to her arms to prevent her from falling forward. He shouldn't have been so close. In that instant, he reacted as if she was still his. He closed his eyes and inhaled her scent, savoring the shape of her arms under his hands.

With a twist, she was out of his reach. Her breathing made her shoulders rise and fall in quick succession. "I never changed my name. I'm a Bergmann, and we don't forget. And we sure don't forgive easily. So, you will call me Ms. Bergmann. No one knows I married you, and it will stay that way."

With the precision of a general, she turned and marched to the small house. He followed. He had a feeling he would follow her to his death if she let him.

Sometimes when something was broken, fixing it wasn't an option. The best a person could do was throw it away and move on. *God, is this where You wanted me, or am I being a stubborn fool?*

Chapter Two

The patrol car slowed down in what looked to be the middle of nowhere, surrounded by nothing. Perfect place for activities that needed to be hidden from the law. Except they found this one.

"Is it safe for you to be out here?" He didn't like the idea of her being around these kinds of lowlifes, the kind that made up his family.

With a quick glare, she gave him his answer loud and clear. It left a bitter burn in his gut to see the hostility coming from eyes that used to look on him with love.

They followed the county car down a narrow, overgrown dirt road. It was another five or six miles deep into the wooded ranch before they came up to a fortress-like structure. Who would want a home that looked like a prison on the outside?

Once through the gate, a building that looked more like a Malibu beach house appeared before them. Several different types of law enforcement were coming in and out of the house. Boxes and computers were being loaded into vans.

Cold sweat broke out over Reid's entire body, and his skin shrunk around his bones. Three breaths in and one long exhale helped a little. They were not here for him. They weren't taking him back to the small windowless concrete cell. He was free and not doing anything that would put him back there.

"Reid? Are you okay?" Hearing her voice calmed him better than all his coping techniques and self-induced pep talks.

Trying to give her a reassuring smile, he

nodded. "Just a few too many uniforms with weapons for my peace of mind."

Officer Bolton tapped her window and waited for her to roll it down. "Dr. Ortiz is right behind us. I'll find out the location of the animals so you can park the trailer close."

She opened the door. "I'll come with you. I have a couple of questions before we enter the area with the jaguar and bear." Over her shoulder, she talked to Reid. "Wait here. When I get the information, can you move the trailer up to the area we'll be exiting with the animals?"

With a nod, he got out of the truck and moved to the driver's side. A few of the officers glanced at him. He kept his head down and counted his breaths.

The ex-con label would be attached to him until the day he died and beyond. He gritted his teeth. It would be part of his life forever now, so he'd better get used to it.

Nothing new. Every male in his family

carried the stigma. Being the only one to finish high school hadn't saved him from his family tradition. He popped his knuckles. Could they tell by looking at him?

Before he hid inside the cab, a large white truck with several compartments in the back pulled up next to him. A tall Hispanic woman stepped out. She came straight to Reid with an inviting grin and her hand out. Reid had to wonder if she bleached her teeth or if they were naturally so white and perfect.

"Hi, I'm Sandra Ortiz. I'm Danica's on-call veterinarian. Since I've never met you, I'm hoping she finally found a vet tech with an animal husbandry degree."

"Reid McAllister. Yes, I'm her new vet tech. For now."

The woman's smile went bigger as they shook hands. "Good, good. I told her not to worry. God would provide."

Reid wasn't sure if it was God or his selfish desire, but he didn't say anything.

"Hey, Sandy." Danica returned and gave the other woman a quick hug. "Seems we have a full-grown male jaguar and a very young bear cub in the basement."

With quick, efficient motions, the vet started pulling equipment from the back of her truck. "Congratulations on the new vet tech. I'll call Gloria and let her know to close the search."

"Oh, no. Don't do that. Reid is one of James's parolees. He's here temporarily, so the faster I can get someone in full-time the better."

Reid saw it. The friendliness turned to suspicion the second the doctor learned she was talking with a convicted criminal. He needed to get used to it.

Every time he started over, people would know, and he'd be an ex-con for the rest of his life. An ex-con without a home or family.

Danica loaded the rifle with the dart Dr. Ortiz had prepared, taking careful aim at the black jaguar as it paced and growled in the small enclosure. There were white patches of hair sprinkled over his coat, indications of old wounds and injuries.

They would have to move fast once she shot him. Anger welled up at the humans who had caged this beautiful wild animal and removed his front claws. His fangs were coated with gold, and a gaudy diamond collar was too snug around his neck. One of his hind legs was not bearing weight.

They'd already removed the young bear cub. She was small enough for Reid to carry her to the large crate secured in the trailer. He now hung back from the other men. Backed into a dark corner, much like the young bear they'd found huddled in her cage.

"Is she going to shoot the cat through the bars of the cage?" She couldn't see who Reid asked, but her husband's low voice caressed her skin.

It had taken her almost two years to get

him out of her mind. She stopped missing him four years ago, but it seemed as if parts of her heart had already forgotten she didn't love him anymore.

She sighed. "Some of us are working over here if you don't mind. The big guy is already scared, and I want to make him as comfortable as possible." Bringing the rifle back to her shoulder, she cast the big cat in her sight. As soon as she pulled the trigger, the jaguar snapped at the spot she hit on his rump. It didn't take him long to go down.

"We need to move fast."

Reid didn't hesitate a minute. He attacked each of the steps like a pro. Dr. Ortiz was working right alongside him as he finished securing a cloth over the animal's eyes to keep the cat calm when he woke. With James and a couple other men, they lifted the cat onto a long board and carried him out.

The entire time, Reid talked in a quiet voice to the animal while they moved him.

The same voice that calmed her when she was upset or stressed.

First thing in the morning, she would start calling her contacts and get the application to the National Wildlife Federation turned in ASAP. She needed to get Reid out of her life, the sooner, the better.

With the animals secured, Reid disappeared inside the truck as she went to touch base with the lead officer.

Unfortunately, he was waiting for her with three more crates. The day was not quite over. She would be leaving with more than the two in the trailer. "The animals are secured. The basement is all yours. What do you have there?"

"Goats. Six kids. We crated them so you could load them quickly." He smiled as if they were a gift.

James came up behind her and touched her arm. "I'll help you with these. I know time is sensitive." He picked up the one closest to him, and the two goats inside started bleating.

Reid joined them. "Is everything okay?" He kept his gaze on her, ignoring the FBI agent.

"Seems as if we have a few more additions to our family. Baby goats." She looked from the FBI agent Reid was avoiding to the crated goats. "Reid, place them in the bed of the truck. There are bungees in the back seat."

With a quick nod, he went to work.

A short time later she drove over the hills, back to her struggling sanctuary, with six baby goats, a black bear cub, an old jaguar and one secret husband in tow.

How had this become her life?

God, I'm working on turning this worry over to You, but right now I'm feeling a bit overwhelmed. Lord, please show me what to do!

"Did you say something?" Reid kept

looking over his shoulder, to the cargo they were hauling.

She didn't think she said anything out loud. Great. Now she was mumbling to herself. "Just having a conversation with God. The babies are safe. No one will get out."

"What about the jaguar? The tranquilizer will wear off soon." He looked back again, his brow furrowed.

"Reid, this isn't my first rodeo. I know what I'm doing. We might have to sedate the big guy again before we can unload him. I've gotten good at working with wild animals, and I know how unpredictable they can be. I promise I've got this under control."

"The bear looks too young to be away from her mother. Will you have to hand-raise her?"

"Yes, but we'll keep hands off as much as possible. She'll be assigned a number. Once she's old enough, we'll either release her into the wild or the bear section on the ranch.

You were great, by the way. Some people have a hard time working with the big animals, even when they're out."

"I learned to work fast while staying calm. It's the best way to survive when you have a two-thousand-pound bull that needs medical attention. I've never been this close to a big cat. He's stunning."

"He's a beauty." This didn't seem real. She was sitting with the man she married six years ago, talking as if he hadn't walked out on her and their daughters. She glanced at him. He was checking the trailer again. "Why did you move close to my hometown? Did you know I was living here?"

"You were always close to your family, and I couldn't imagine you being away from your twin sister for too long. When we talked about the future, it involved Clear Water and your family. So even if you hadn't moved back home, I knew you would be around. I meant it when I said I hadn't planned on blindsiding you like this." He turned to face her. His gray-green eyes scanned her face before coming back to meet her gaze.

With a sharp breath, she turned her focus on the rural highway. Just because Reid's eyes still did things to her insides didn't mean it was wise to trust him. That was more evidence that she needed to be wary and keep her distance.

"But why even come back to the Hill Country? Why not New Orleans or Houston? Don't you have family in both of those places?" It would have been so much better if he stayed away. She had gotten good at the out-of-sight-out-of-mind game she played with herself.

"None that I want to claim. There's nothing in Houston or New Orleans for me other than trouble. While in prison, I met Ray Martinez. His church had a prison ministry and organized Bible studies. He changed my life. Well, God used him to change me."

Her jaw started to hurt, making her take a deep breath to relax. The resentment burning in her gut would turn toxic if she allowed it to fester. "I tried to get you to church the whole time we were dating. You were always too busy." Sarcasm might not be the best option, but it made her feel better. "So, you found God in prison, and now you want to right all your wrongs?"

"It's not that easy."

He was fortunate she didn't throw things at him. Hand over hand, she turned off the highway onto the farm-to-market road that led to the sanctuary. Silence lingered, and she let it hang between them. She needed to focus on the hurt and abused animals and her daughters. She had to figure out what would be best for them.

Pulling up to the large gate, she rolled down her window. The Texas heat hit her. It felt good in contrast with the coldness of the cab. Leaning out the window, she punched in the code for the gate. The gate paused halfway. She hit the box, and it started moving again. She needed someone to look at the motor. Maybe her baby sister would do it for free.

Dr. Ortiz followed along with Reid's parole officer. Her long-lost husband had a parole officer. There was no reason for him to know about the twins, and her innocent girls didn't have to find out their father was a convict.

Once parked, they all got out and sedated the cat again. As a team, they moved fast to get the cat in an exam room so Sandy could check him. There was an old break in his hind leg that they wouldn't be able to correct. Bruises and small cuts covered his body. While the vet and Danica tended to the big guy, Reid stayed at the jaguar's head the whole time, keeping him calm and watching for signs of stress.

Removing the gold caps from the deadly fangs, Sandy shook her head. "I just don't understand people. Taking a beautiful animal and turning him into a freak show for their warped entertainment."

Lowering the table, they slid him into an enormous wooden crate. As Danica closed the door, the cat lashed out and caught the edge of Reid's hand with its teeth.

Once Danica secured the latch, she grabbed his hand. Without asking, she pulled him to the sink. "I don't think it needs stitches." She glanced at Dr. Ortiz. "What do you think?"

Reid tensed under her touch as they crowded around his minuscule injury. She glanced up and found him staring off at the crated cat. "Are you okay?"

He jerked his chin. "I've had much worse."

Sandy went to the cabinets and came back with ointments and bandages. "It's not deep. I think you'll just need to keep it clean and bandaged for a few days."

"After checking the cub, we'll need to fill out an incident report." Danica kept her head down.

Both women worked on his hand. At one point, he tried to pull back. His free hand rubbed his forehead. "It was my fault. You don't need to write him up. He was scared, and we all have the instinct to protect ourselves."

He didn't flinch once while they worked on the cut. "The cat's not going to get in trouble." She carefully added the small metal clip to hold the wrap in place. "But I do have to write up the incident. Not following the rules is what gets us in trouble. Hiding the truth doesn't help anyone." Her voice grew a little stronger than it needed to be.

Sandy gave Reid a hard look. "We can't put the refuge at risk because of a simple documentation you don't want to take the time to fill out."

Reid rolled his neck and looked down, a frown on his face. This wasn't Sandy's fight, so Danica wasn't sure what happened to the vet's usual friendly manner. Possibly she was having a tough day. Danica could relate to that. Instead of wasting time trying to figure out other people's problems, she went to the baby bear.

The small black bear looked healthy, except for being a little underweight and hungry. Sandy filled out the health form. "He'll need to be hand-fed for now."

The little bear seemed to have bonded with Reid, wanting to cling to him. Danica went into the kitchen area to fix her a bottle. Sandy followed her.

"I need to go. I'll take the new guy with me and drop him off wherever he belongs. Or I could take him to Bobby."

"He's fine. It's been a while since we had a baby of this type, so I need Reid to help prep the enclosure."

"I don't think that's wise. I'd stay, but I need to finish my rounds. He's not staying here, is he?" Disgust dripped from each word.

Danica stopped mixing the formula and looked at Sandy. "No, he has a job as a wrangler at the Hausman ranch. What's wrong with you? We use parolees all the time."

"All the others stayed with Bobby to get their hours. Are you so naive that you don't worry about being alone with an ex-con? Worse, as a vet tech he has access to everything in the office and will be spending most of his time with you. Alone. You just met him today. Do you even know what he did?" Her friend and vet looked more vexed than she had ever seen. She stood with her arms crossed.

"James Bolton is his parole officer. He wouldn't bring a dangerous convict out here. The charge was transporting drugs."

Sandy's eyes went wide. "You have a drug dealer in here. Do you realize some of the drugs kept here have high street value?"

Danica tried to stop the eye roll, but she wasn't sure she was entirely successful. Sandy didn't know how well she knew Reid. "I'm not stupid enough to trust him. Yes, he's an ex-con, and yes, I have everything of value locked away. I need his expertise to get my paperwork finished and filed. As soon as you find me a vet tech with the right degree, he's gone." Thrusting her hip out, she pointed to her walkie-talkie. "Bobby is one click away."

Reid cleared his throat from the doorway. The cub curled in his arms, lying against his chest, sound asleep. Her traitorous heart thought of him holding their daughters. Heat caused her skin to burn. "Reid—"

"A girl named Sarah is here. She said to let you know she's feeding the orphaned bats." His eyes looked more gray than green before he returned to the other room.

Sandy stepped in front of Danica as she started following Reid. "Now, don't go feeling sorry for him. He's a criminal. You know I've always been uncomfortable with having the parolees out here."

The need to apologize ate at her. "He's a human who is trying to do the right thing."

"You've known him one day. That man is

not one of your rescue projects. He's a grown adult that knows right from wrong, and he chose wrong."

"You don't know him."

"Neither do you. Unfortunately, I do know men like him. He'll get what he wants and leave you smashed and bleeding. When he's taken everything he needs, he'll walk out without a backward glance." Sandy reached out and took the bottle from her. "Trust me. I know what I'm talking about. I'll get this to Sarah. When I leave, I'll take the con with me."

Danica took the bottle back. "Thank you for the warning, but I've got this. You can go. I'll have Bobby take Reid back to the Hausman Ranch. By the way, he has a name. Reid. And just like my animals, he deserves to be treated with respect. Okay?"

She sighed. "You sure you got this?"

"Yes." She laid her hand on Sandy's arm. "Thank you for caring, but I know what I'm doing."

With a grunt, Sandy shook her head. "Those words almost guarantee impending doom."

Going into the other room, they found Reid in the rocking chair. The cub was still asleep curled up in his arms. Danica grabbed the long leather gloves and prepared to feed the new baby. Sandy glared at Reid. "I'll be back out tomorrow to do a follow-up. Will you be back?"

He nodded. "I have the early shift at the ranch, so I'll be here at two o'clock."

The vet turned to Danica. "I'll be here at two. We can evaluate if the big guy is ready for release and do a follow-up with the little one." With one last hostile stare at Reid, Sandy left.

Danica sighed and reached for the bear. The smell of the formula in the bottle had her awake and making noises. She couldn't help but laugh at her antics. "Poor baby is hungry."

A loud rumble came from Reid's stomach.

She raised a brow. "Are you needing to be fed, too? When did you eat last?"

His golden tan skin flushed a bit. He shook his head and kept his eyes focused on the bear.

"Reid. When did you eat last?"

He shrugged. "We had an early breakfast at the ranch."

Knowing ranch life, that would have been before sunup. "It's after four! Why didn't you say something?" The bear finished the last of the mixture.

"Sorry. Making my own decisions still feels odd. After six years, I got used to others telling me what to do and when to do it. Some habits are hard to shake."

That made her heart break a little. She remembered the carefree young man who loved being outdoors, riding bulls, drawing and poetry. She fell so hard in love with him. But like Sandy said, she didn't know this Reid.

She wanted to know why he did it. Why

Reid gave up on them so quickly. If they had worked hard, they could have made it. He hadn't had enough faith in them. "I have some sandwich stuff in the refrigerator."

The bear moved and crawled up his leg, trying to get under his shirt. "Are you going to give her a new name? Her collar said Slasher." He gently pulled her out and hugged the bear close. "I don't like that name."

"With the intent to keep them wild, we have a policy not to humanize them. She'll be assigned a number for her file, but no name. You shouldn't hold her so much."

"Babies need to be held. So she'll get a number? Will she spend the night in the crate?"

Taking the cub out of his arms, she put her back into the wooden structure. They placed blankets and a floppy stuffed bear for her to cuddle. "After I feed you, we can clean and prep a large enclosure we made a couple of years ago for two orphaned bears. She'll live there until we can release her in the bear habitat. If we do this right, she could be a candidate for release into the wild. We don't want her to rely on humans too much."

With the baby tucked away, she went to the central building. One of the volunteer college students was doing homework while covering their twenty-four-hour hotline. "Hi, Diego. This is Reid McAllister. He's our new vet tech." The men shook hands. "Is Sarah still here?"

"She was bathing the bats a minute ago."

She introduced Reid to Sarah and the orphaned bats, then headed to the kitchen. Digging in the refrigerator she found enough supplies to make two sandwiches. They finished their meal in silence.

There were a hundred ways to start a conversation with her secret husband, but she needed to keep it professional until he left for good. With empty plates in the sink, they went outside. They got in her favorite ATV, a double-seated four-wheeler that looked like a golf cart on steroids. The large enclosure was deep in the ranch.

"What happened?" Reid pointed to the old homestead as they passed it, a ranch house built in 1918.

"When Linda, the owner, was moved to full-time care, the house caught fire. It was small, and it just took out the back room, but it did enough damage that it would take lots of money to restore it. It had been her plan that the caretaker of the sanctuary would live there."

"Aren't you the caretaker?" His gaze moved from the turn-of-the-century old rock home to her.

She blinked. Another dream put aside. She had planned to move out of her father's house with the girls, but for now, she was grateful they had a safe place to live. "Yeah, but all the available funds have gone into the direct care of the animals." She sighed. "I always wanted to. Maybe someday." But at this rate, she doubted it. When did faith turn into stubbornness? Would she even be able to tell the difference?

As the enclosure came into view, Bobby waved. He had already started pulling the old bedding out. She parked and got off the cart with Reid to join Bobby. With the three of them working, it didn't take long to get the chain-fence enclosure ready for the newest baby on the ranch. Reid stood in the center after they finished, sweating. He had dragged a large tree branch that was knocked down in the last storm. "Where do you want this?"

"We can tie it to the corner post and the stand. It will give her something natural to climb on and sleep in if she wants. From here, she can also get in the hammock, too."

A small book fell from Reid's pocket when he bent over to grab at the tree again. Without thinking, she reached down, and they bumped heads. "Sorry." She picked up the leather book. It was a Bible. "You carry a Bible with you now?"

He took it and grunted.

She looked down and noticed a couple of yellow ribbons had slipped from his pocket, as well. "Oh, Reid."

In college, he'd told her the story behind them. She had cried for the little boy that thought his father would come back home if he tied the yellow ribbons outside. He had heard the song "Tie a Yellow Ribbon Around the Old Oak Tree" and truly believed it.

It took her back to her childhood, when she desperately wanted her mother to come home, but she was dead. At five, she hadn't understood.

"You still have those?"

"They're just bookmarks." He stuffed them back into the Bible. "They don't mean anything."

"Reid, that's not—" Her phone vibrated. She glanced at the screen.

Oh, no. It was later than she'd thought. Turning away from Reid and Bobby, Danica spoke with her father. "Sorry, Daddy. We had some emergency arrivals, and I lost track of time."

Along with a long-lost husband showing up on her doorstep. With a quick glance over her shoulder, she found Bobby showing Reid some of the things they made for the bears.

Her father was talking, and she needed to focus. "Yes, let them know I have a great story to tell when I get home. I'll be there in the next hour... No, don't— Hey, girls." She moved farther away and lowered her voice. "That's right. I promise to tell you everything... Yes, I'll take pictures... Okay. Love you more."

Bobby looked at her with one brow raised. "Everything good?"

"Yes." She put her phone away. "I just forgot to tell Daddy we had new arrivals. He expected me home a couple of hours ago."

"Did you tell the g—"

She cut the facility manager off before he

could mention her twins. "I think it's time to call it a night. Reid, I can drive you to the ranch."

"That's nonsense." Bobby's gruff voice told her what he thought of her being alone with Reid. Why did everyone in her life act as if she had no survival instincts? It was getting old.

He rubbed his mustache and adjusted his hat. "I'll take him, and I can pick him up tomorrow."

Reid looked at her like he wanted to say something. He probably had plans to talk more about their little problem when they were alone. Maybe it would be better for Bobby to take him, because she couldn't handle more alone time with her husband.

Sandy was right about him breaking her heart. What the other woman didn't know was that it was already too late. Her heart was left in bloody pieces six years ago. Her daughters were the one thing that forced her to pull herself up and move on with life. Now it was up to her to protect their innocent hearts.

Chapter Three

"How long have you been out?" Bobby turned down the backcountry road that would take them to Danica. Hopefully, the second day of his return would fare better than the first.

"Not long." He didn't want to talk. He'd rather torment himself with thoughts of his wife.

"How long do you plan to stick around?"

"As long as Dani needs me." He groaned and laid his head back. He had let her nickname slip past his lips.

"I think it would be best if you referred to

her as Ms. Bergmann." They hit a pothole on Reid's side of the truck. Without his seat belt, he would have hit his head.

"Yes, sir." He didn't want to hear another warning to stay away.

The old cowboy found a couple more potholes to hit. They finally made it to the gate. Reid knew he had some new bruises. Bobby winked at him.

As they pulled in behind the old bunkhouse, Danica and Dr. Ortiz were waiting for them. He greeted the doctor as he got out of the truck. A few others joined them. "Reid, this is Stephanie Lee, Linda Edward's niece. She's on the board. She has been an advocate for the dream her aunt had for the ranch. Stephanie, this is Reid McAllister. He saved the day with his degree in animal husbandry. Best of all, he has experience with big animals and wild horses."

"Welcome aboard." In high heels and with perfect hair, she looked more prepared for a day in the courtroom than one spent hanging out with wild animals. Her red lips stretched into a tight smile as she looked him up and down.

Reid tried not to be oversensitive and stood still. He learned fast to always appear confident, even when he didn't feel that way. She reminded him of the court-appointed lawyer who threw him to the wolves and walked away without a care.

Stephanie was a trusted member of Danica's circle, and he wasn't. So he smiled and offered his hand. Yeah, she wasn't happy about touching him.

Danica, who had been speaking with Dr. Ortiz, waved them over. "Dr. Ortiz examined our new cat. The jaguar is in general good health, but the back leg is permanently damaged. We'll release him into the north cat area." She looked at Dr. Ortiz, then at Reid. "Are we ready to move him?"

The wheeled crate was four feet tall and six feet long. Reid could hear the black cat pacing. Working as a team, they loaded him into the back of a trailer and slowly drove out to the cat area in the far back part of the ranch. It took some maneuvering, but they got the crate placed inside a double-fenced area that was free of trees.

By the time they rolled the crate up against the second gate, the sun was high, and the Texas heat had stopped being friendly. Danica had everyone clear the area and stand outside the enclosure. She and Reid were the only people inside, ready to let the cat into his new home. Dr. Ortiz stood next to the tall fence with a tranquilizer if they needed it.

Danica jumped on top of the crate. She looked like an Amazon queen, surveying her land. She was born to do this. Twisting around, she looked at Reid. "I'm going to lift the front panel. He'll either dart out and run, or hide in there. We'll have to wait for him to enter his new world." Easing down, she laid her body flat on the top of the crate and peered into the openings. In a low, sooth-ing voice, she started talking to the animal.

"What do you need me to do?" Reid kept his voice steady and calm as he checked on the black jaguar from the side panel.

"Stay to the back of the crate until he moves out the front. As soon as he leaves, I need you to slide and secure the gate so he can't come back into this area. I'll roll it out of the way."

She sprang to her feet. "By nature, they want to avoid humans, so he should run for the trees. Okay, here we go." Giving Reid a nod, she got in position.

Poised for action, he kept his full attention on her. It would be safer for her on the out-side fence area with the others, but he knew better than to suggest it.

Danica pulled the panel up. Nothing hap-pened. Reid pressed his face against the top slot to see inside. The cat had his nose in the air and took one cautious step toward the opening. Then he stopped and just stared out.

Slowly slipping down to the ground, Danica stood next to him. He was tall, and her lips were close to his ear when she leaned in. "All he's known is captivity, his whole life. The open space probably scares him."

"Freedom can be overwhelming." He had only been locked up six years and was surprised how hard it was to adjust. Facing freedom after a whole life of being in a cage had to be paralyzing.

She nodded. With the palm of her hand, she wiped at her face. Reid pretended not to notice. Her warrior face was back, as she focused on the jaguar.

The cat eased closer to the opening and once again sat and put his nose in the air. He turned around and went to the back of his shelter again.

"No. Go. Run," Danica whispered. "There are rocky cliffs and trees for you to climb and explore. You're safe here."

The cat paced again and stopped at the door. His ears twitched. Reid stopped breathing for a few seconds as he waited for the cat to claim his freedom.

Danica slid her hand into his. Reid heard her praying under her breath. She was so focused on the jag he doubted she even noticed. He resisted the urge to squeeze, hoping she would stay. If this caged and abused wild animal could make it, maybe he had a chance, too.

It took almost an hour for the cat to get his whole body out of the crate. Suddenly he stood straight. With a flip of his tail, he lifted his head high, and his nostrils flared. He looked over his shoulder, then back again. With a lunge, he ran for the tree line.

Danica pulled the crate back. "Lock the gate."

He had gotten so caught up holding her hand and watching the cat, he almost forgot his job. The small group behind them started applauding. The black cat reappeared and darted across the open grass, running straight back into the fence. Panting, he stopped and went flat. Danica held her hand up, and everyone went silent.

Reid hated seeing the big cat in distress. "Should we let him back in the crate? He doesn't feel safe in the open space."

With narrowed eyes, she kept her focus on the cat. "He's okay. Let's give him a bit more time." The animal's golden eyes scanned the land. Lying flat on his stomach, he crept back to the tree line.

One swish of his tail and he turned back to the trees. One leap and he climbed onto the low branch of a giant oak. Danica looked at him with a huge smile. "I think he's going to adjust fast." Hands on the crate, she unlocked the brakes and started rolling it toward the volunteers. They rushed forward to help her.

"That was so exciting, Ms. Bergmann. Will he be able to find the water and his food?"

"I think so. We'll keep an eye on him to make sure he does. The more he does on his own, the better." Danica gave the small crew directions. Dr. Ortiz hugged her, then got in her fancy vet truck and left.

Reid stood back. They all laughed and talked about the excitement of setting the cat free. Everyone had a job and knew what to do. A touch on his left shoulder caused him to spin with his fists up for a split second before he saw it was Danica. "Sorry." He stuffed his hands in his back pockets. "I didn't know you were behind me." He hated the pity that clouded her eyes.

"I didn't even think about how—"

"I'm fine. What do you need me to do?" Relaxing his jaw, he focused on his breathing. Once back to normal, he looked down at the beautiful woman who had looked at him with love a lifetime ago. The tender gaze was gone—now it shifted from suspicion to pity. She had a don't-get-close look he'd never seen before.

Even though he was free now, he felt as if he'd suffered a lifetime conviction. Ray said it was a self-induced sentence, which God had released him from. Now that he had his physical freedom, all the guilt and stress were back. He didn't feel free anymore.

"Reid?" Her bright green eyes searched his face. He forced himself to be still, to meet her gaze. She gave him a sad smile and nodded as if they had agreed to something he wasn't aware of. "Are you ready to move the baby cub to the enclosure? I don't want a crowd for that."

Right now, he would love to get away from this group of young, energetic college students. It seemed a lifetime ago that he had been a part of that life. If he heard the words *awesome* or *amazing* one more time, he was going to beat his head against the side of the truck.

Then there was Bobby. The old man eyed Reid with a warning whenever he got a chance. "Is there anything else needed done here?"

"Are you sure you're okay?" Her forehead wrinkled with worry, and it was his fault.

With a nod, he gave her the lopsided grin she'd always loved. "Yes. Ready for the next adventure."

She waved to the others. "We're heading back to introduce the cub to her new home. Y'all take the truck. Sarah, do you have the phone today?"

"Yes, ma'am. Can we come watch?"

"I want to keep the environment calm and quiet when we make the transition. I need y'all to finish here and do the usual rounds. We'll take the four-wheeler back to headquarters." Without waiting for him, she jumped on the long leather seat of the ATV. Hands on the handlebars, she leaned forward, making room for him behind her. If he got on that thing, he would have to touch her. Not good.

"Baby, I'll walk."

"What? It'll take you an hour to get back." She started the engine. "Do you want to drive? Is that the problem? I don't remember you being so macho."

Okay, he was making a bigger deal out of this than it needed to be. Swinging a leg over, he slid as far back on the seat as possible. Trying to settle in behind Danica, he found there wasn't much room to avoid her. Her hair was in a tight braid, but a few curls had managed to escape. He could get lost in her hair. Looking to the sky, he kept his focus on the clouds above. His hands gripped the bars next to his legs. A rock in the road caused the four-wheeler to tilt to the side.

Without thought, his fingers immediately circled her waist to steady them both. Muscles briefly contracted as he remembered how perfectly she fit in his hands. Those hands needed to be somewhere else.

One quick movement and he had a tight grip on the bars again. Those were the kind of memories that would get him in trouble and just cause him more pain. He needed to block all of them.

How could he do that? He remembered everything about her, and he would until the day his heart stopped beating. He imagined it was possible that even beyond this life, he would remember her. Not that it would do him any good. He was dancing in the middle of a stampede and would be going down soon.

This quick ride turned into a torture trip. Next time, he would walk. *God, I need strength only You can give. I have vowed to do the right thing, but I'm not sure I'm strong enough.*

Parking the four-wheeler by the back door, Danica jumped off as fast as she turned the key to shut down the engine. She needed to get away from Reid.

Driving with him so close, it took her back to the early days of their marriage. Their very short marriage, because he didn't have enough faith to believe God would take care of them.

"I need to check something up front. Go ahead and get the cub ready."

Not waiting for his response, she moved to the front porch. She had to get herself under control. Emotions and feelings had gotten her in trouble in college. Now she was a grown woman with two innocent baby girls relying on her. Their future was at stake. *God, I need You to lead me this time.*

It didn't matter how Reid McAllister made her feel. Her heart was off-limits, and she needed to use her brain. Coming around the corner, she stopped midstep. No, no, no.

"Momma!"

"Momma, we came to see the baby bear."

The girls charged at her. "We want to see the bats. Can we see the bats? Are they sleeping like little burritos?"

There was no pause between the girls. They had a habit of talking with their words flowing from one sister to the next.

Her gaze darted behind her. Reid had gone into the building. With her heart in her throat, she stared at her twin sister. "Jackie, what are you doing here? I told the girls I would bring them later tonight."

Jackie narrowed her gaze. "What's going on?"

With another quick glance to the house, she took a deep breath. Maybe she could get them out of here without him seeing the girls. She bit her lip.

"Momma, please."

Or before her sister saw him. This was crazy. Smiling for the girls, she took a deep breath. No time to drown in her own mess.

Balancing on her heels, she squatted and hugged each girl. "I need you to go home with your aunt." She pushed the loose curls out of their faces, their red hair and gray-green eyes in contrast to their light golden skin.

They were a perfect mix of her and Reid. "You can't be here right now. I promise I'll bring you back, and you can help me feed the baby bats tonight." She usually only allowed the girls to watch the bats. At this point, she was willing to use anything to get them back in the big green family Suburban her father still owned. Standing, she placed a hand on each of the girls' shoulders and started herding them back to the SUV.

Jackie was frowning at her. "They both got a hundred on their spelling tests, so I thought this—"

"It's fine. I just need you to take them home. I still have a lot to do today."

A door behind her opened. Her sister gasped. Dread froze the rapid flow of her blood. Fear held her in place. Her two worlds were about to collide. "Please, get the twins to the car and leave." *Please, please, please don't let him notice the girls.*

"Jackie?" His deep voice vibrated down her spine.

"Reid?" Jackie's screech was more like

nails on a chalkboard. Eyes wide, she looked at Danica. "Is that Reid McAllister?"

The girls turned to see the newcomer. "Hi!" They tended to talk in unison when they were excited. "I'm Susan Bergmann this is my sister—"

"Elizabeth Bergmann. Everyone calls us Suzie and Lizzy. We're twins."

Focusing on her daughters, she kept her back to Reid. Maybe he'd assume they were Jackie's if he didn't look too close.

Lizzy gently pressed her fingertips on Danica's face and pulled her attention away from Jackie. "Momma, please let us just see the bats. We won't touch them."

She groaned and closed her eyes.

"Or even make a noise. We promise to be real quiet." On her other side, Suzie wrapped herself around Danica's arm.

"Yes, we'll be good." They both looked past her and smiled at Reid. "Have you seen the bats?" Suzie faced him.

"We were here when they came to the

sanctuary." Excitement bubbled from each of Lizzy's words.

"They were the size of our thumbs." Both girls held up their thumbs and giggled.

Danica's lungs burned. She took in a deep breath. She needed to breathe. Passing out was not an option. On second thought, it would be a great distraction and buy her some time.

She finally turned to face Reid. His gaze was on the girls, darting back and forth between her wiggling, joy-filled babies. Lizzy had grabbed her hand. "Momma, please just one peek."

Tearing her gaze away from the shock on Reid's face, she looked down. "Sweetheart, we have some real important things going on right now. I need you to go home with Aunt Jackie. I'll bring you back tonight for the late-night feeding."

Jackie stepped forward and took the girls by the hand. "Come on, sugars. The sooner your mom gets her work done, the faster she'll come get you." She glanced at Reid, then back to Danica. "Are you okay? Do I need to call anyone?"

"No. Really, I'm good. Reid is here to help." Crossing her arms, she swallowed back any tears that would expose the desperation she was trying to hide. "Call me once you're in the car if you want, and I'll let you know when to expect me."

Her sister hesitated. "Bobby's here?"

"Yes, along with Stephanie and a couple of interns. We just released the cat, lots of people are here. I'm good."

Watching her daughters leave with her sister, her gut burned. Maybe he'd go away if she ignored him. She felt him move next to her. His breathing was hard enough to brush her unprotected neck. Closing her eyes, she prayed, with every bit of energy in her body. If she could, she would drop to her knees.

She did not want to deal with this.

"I'm a father? Why didn't—"

She turned on him, her fingertip against

his chest. "You, Reid McAllister, are not a father. You made me a mother, then you left. That does not make you a father. Don't you dare try to act like the victim here." Heat ran through her limbs.

Devastation flared in his eyes. Years ago, he shared dreams of forging a family with her, the type of family he had only seen on television. Reid had talked about being the kind of father he'd wanted to be, a good father. He'd wanted to do things differently than his parents.

At the time, she was foolish enough to believe him.

Danica stared him down, the gray in his eyes glossed over until only a dark green burned. So let him get angry. She didn't care. Her rage heaved and pulled against the shackles she'd locked it under years ago.

Her finger thrust against his rock-hard chest. "I waited for you." Her voice shook. She squared her shoulders. "When I took the first pregnancy test, I was alone. I've been alone every step of the way, except for my family. My girls are Bergmanns, and that's all they know. You showing up on my doorstep does not change the fact they don't have a father. They never did, and they're fine, better than fine. They have my father. The kind of man I want them to know."

Mouth open, he didn't say a word. Deep in the back of his throat, his voice emerged. "They're mine."

"No. You gave up that right when you decided it was easier just to vanish than tell me what was happening. I'm not talking to you about them." Unable to deal with his self-inflicted wounds any longer, she marched past him and into the office. Slamming the door felt better than it should.

She didn't have time for this drama or his wounded pride. "He should have thought of that before he drove a suspicious car across state lines."

"Who are you talking to?"

Stephanie's voice caused her to jump. She

forced a laugh. "Just myself." She looked around. "Where is everyone? What are you doing in my office?"

"Oh, they're putting everything away, and Sarah is checking on the bats. I wanted to get the updates on the paperwork." She leaned her perfectly dressed hip on the corner of the worn, outdated desk. "How are we looking financially?"

Danica moved past her and bit down on the inside of her cheek. This was not what she wanted to deal with right now. "We have a board meeting soon. I'll be able to give a full report then."

"I spoke with Dorothy. As your friends and board members, we're worried. Do we have enough money to hire a vet tech?" Stephanie started looking through some photos Danica had taken for the grant. "He's a convicted criminal. Is it smart to have him around so many drugs and exotic animals?"

"He needs community hours, and we need him for the grant. James trusts him. Sorry I don't have time to go deeper, but I have lots of work that still needs to be done before the end of the day."

Her temper was on the edge of exploding, but it wasn't Stephanie's fault. Plus, she really couldn't afford to be rude to her. Not only was she Linda's only living relative, but she stood by her side as a major advocate for the sanctuary.

"I'm sorry. I know your aunt's dream for this place is as important to you as it is to me. But right now, I don't have time. I promise I have a report, and I will answer all of your questions then." She took a breath. "Thank you for helping today. I know you also have a busy schedule with your law firm."

"Danica, are we going to move the cub?" Reid stood at her door. He wasn't looking at her, though. He seemed to be staring at Stephanie.

"Seems the felon needs you. Shouldn't leave him unattended for long. I have to go anyway. I'll see you at the board meeting." She ignored Reid as she went out the other door.

Danica swallowed, or tried to anyway. The ball of fear and worry hung in her dry throat. She shouldn't have rushed Stephanie out. Maybe she could call Bobby, so someone would be between her and Reid.

"I'll be with the cub." Not giving her a chance to reply, Reid turned on his booted heel and left.

Bracing her hands on the edge of the desk, she hung her head. "God, please give me the wisdom to handle this the best way for the girls." Her wounded heart wanted to lash out at him and make him pay, but that wouldn't help anyone. As good as it would feel to scream and throw breakables against his head, she knew it would just destroy her in the long haul. More guilt was the last thing she needed right now.

With a deep breath, she turned to face the door leading to Reid and the baby bear.

There was no reason for her to feel guilty. For six years, she'd stayed strong. God had been preparing her for this day. Danica swallowed any emotions that might give him an opening to her heart and stepped into the room with her husband.

Chapter Four

Reid held the bottle as the baby bear clung to him. He took a deep breath, pushing his lungs past their comfort zone. Releasing all the tension, he counted to five. Held it. Again.

It wasn't working.

No matter how he tried to center his breathing, the word *daughters* bounced around in his head. The double image of the most beautiful sight he'd ever seen ricocheted in his thoughts.

Two curly-red-haired girls. He had two daughters with the same color of eyes as his mother. Two daughters who were already five years old. Five years he could never get back. Anger threatened to abolish all his good intentions.

Danica was right. He'd walked out on her when she needed him most. He'd ruined his own life. A life that not only shined with Danica as his wife but two precious girls who...

His family had ridiculed him for trying to make a better life, for reaching over his head for things that belonged to other people. Not him.

The night he was arrested they had been proven right. There was no escaping his family blood.

But daughters? What did he do with that information? Even after seeing them, he still couldn't believe it. He wanted to yell and hit something.

He stroked the bear's fur and looked down, into her trusting eyes. Centering his thoughts and turning to God was what he needed to do now.

As much as he wanted to blame Danica, he couldn't. The mistake was his, and now he had a great deal to prove to her.

The rocking chair creaked as it rolled back and forth. Reid leaned his head back. The peeling paint on the old wood panel revealed decades of colors just painted on top of each other. It needed to be sanded and repainted. No one had ever taken the time to do the job right. Layers of paint had been slapped onto each other, covering the old stains.

If she had the supplies to make repairs, he could work on restoring the old wood. Words were not going to regain the trust he'd lost. It was going to take a lot of work and time to show her he could be counted on.

His mother had put her husband above her children. Each time his father got out of prison, his mother took him back, no questions asked. A corner of his lip twitched as he looked down at the bear. "Danica made it clear I wasn't getting anywhere near her babies. I think she might be the definition of mama bear."

"Are you talking to the bear?" Not making eye contact, Danica marched across the room. She gave no indication she had actually heard what he said.

"No one else will talk to me."

A snort came from her as she pulled bottles and assorted supplies out of the cabinets. "When you finish with the feeding, we'll move her out to the enclosure." With jerky fast motions, she stuffed them in the bag. "I'll wait in the Jeep that's parked out back." Without a glance at him, she flung the bag over her back and left.

Standing, he cleared his thoughts and prepared himself for her proximity again. He didn't want to put the bear back in the traveling crate, so he carried her out the door.

With the bear sleeping like a baby in his arms, he joined a silent Danica and carefully closed the door. Slowly, she maneuvered the

Jeep over uneven roads. By the time she put the vehicle in Park, the sun was low on the horizon. In the far side of the sky, a large moon was already making its climb.

Taking a moment to collect his thoughts, Reid sat in the Jeep. The moon was one of many little things he'd taken for granted before he was locked up. In his arms, the sleeping cub made a few grunting noises. He wondered how his babies slept. Did they snore? Did they wake up all through the night or sleep without a care in the world?

Monumental everyday life moments he'd lost forever.

The gate to the closed-in area was wide-open. Reid got out of the Jeep and walked into the bear's new home, closing the gate behind him. It was a hundred times larger than the cage in the basement. Even bigger than his cell.

Danica stopped in front of the Jeep and went through her bag. "It won't take long to get her settled. Then I'll have Bobby take you home." Busy movements took her around the enclosure and into a shed that was a few feet away. Finally, she stilled and stood a distance from the fence as if afraid of him.

A pressure tightened in the center of his chest. He pushed past it and cleared his throat. "We need to talk."

Danica had all the power here, and she knew it. His heart twisted. She made it clear she was going to ignore him as she checked the bag again.

"I'm not asking you to tell them I'm their father." He needed to find a way to explain his intentions. *God, help me.* This was tough. The desire to run and hide pulled on every nerve. But he needed to take a stand and face what he feared. "I want to know them. An opportunity to show you I can be trusted. I want a chance to—"

"No!"

He pressed his lips tight. She was the mother of his children. The kind of mother who would protect her children from the corruption in the world, even if that included him.

Danica was so much stronger than his mother.

"Danica. I know I messed up." He moved to the hammock, planning to place the small cub into the cocoon. It was easier to talk to her if he didn't make eye contact. "I took something precious, and I crushed it." The bear's eyes went half-mast. He made sure to relax his hold and regulate his breathing. "But I've seen our girls. I can't undo that." Steel chains seized his lungs, and his eyes burned. "Tell me what you want, and I'll do it. Just let me see them. They don't have to know who I am. I understand you're protecting them. I…" He couldn't even express how much that meant to him.

"Because of you, I'm stronger than I ever thought I could be. You leaving forced me to be independent and focus on what matters. I didn't have the luxury to fall apart."

She crossed her arms as if a chill had swept through her.

The hills to the west received her full attention. "The pain you caused? It hurt beyond what I thought possible to survive. I lost my mother, my grandparents. My oldest sister had left us, and then you, but when I found out about my babies…"

With a tight fist, she tapped her heart. "I had to turn all that pain into faith and love. You broke me, but when I pulled everything back together, I found a woman who can stand on her own. I don't need anyone."

Anger and pride stiffening her spine, Danica looked him straight in the eye. The green irises burned bright, but not with the love he'd remembered for the last six years.

"I can't have you in my life. My daughters don't need a man who will walk out on them without warning. I don't trust you."

The desire to hold Danica, to comfort her, shredded him. He had done this to her. "Danica. I'm sorry."

"You need to let her go. The longer she stays around humans, the harder it will be for her to adjust." She moved back to the Jeep.

"If I had to do it over again, I'd call you and tell you everything. If I got to do it over, I'd never take the job." He eased the baby into the hammock and studied the rescued animal as she settled. "When is their birthday? Tell me that at least."

Hunger for any information about them clawed at his gut. A long heavy pause lingered. Not able to take the silence any longer, he turned. She wasn't even looking at him. She placed her hands on the hood of the white Jeep, gazing out at the surrounding hills.

"Are they in school?" The burn of venom crawled up from the back of his throat. Six years of memories lost. "Danica, they're my daughters. I have some rights. Is my name on their birth certificates?"

Fire flared in her eyes as she grew taller

and marched to the chain-link fence that separated them. A hostile finger pointed at him. "You don't have any rights when it comes to my girls." Her breaths came in quick pants.

A few steps and he stood before her. He gripped the interlocking chains. The edge cut into his skin. "I don't want to fight you, but I can't act as if I don't know that I have children. You know I vowed to be a present father. I have to be a better father than mine."

"Then you should have stayed out of prison I guess." The starch left her spine. Pulling her jacket tight around her, she looked away.

The dying sunlight seemed to set her hair on fire. The shades of golden red radiated warmth. She turned, heading to the Jeep. Reid panicked.

The bear habitat closed in on him. He rattled the fence. "Danica! Don't leave me!"

"I'll call Bobby and tell him to take you

home." She disappeared on the other side of the Jeep.

In his fear, Reid had forgotten he could unlock the gate and walk out. He flipped the latch and followed her. "We have to talk about this."

She kept walking, but it didn't take many steps for him to catch up with her.

Danica held her phone up. Reid assumed she was looking for a signal. Moving to the other side of the road, she paused again. "I'm not even thinking." The walkie-talkie was pulled off her hip. "Bobby, meet us by the bear enclosure. Reid is ready to leave."

"Be there in ten."

He had ten minutes to find out something, anything about his girls. "What do they know about me?"

She climbed into the Jeep, slamming the door. That was it. Danica was going to leave him out here without even the smallest fact about his daughters.

He rushed to open the passenger door. "I

just want to know their birthday. Can I have that much?"

Hands on the wheel, jaw clenched, she turned and glared at him. "They were born February 14. Your very last Valentine's gift to me. Now shut the door."

She turned the key. "Bobby's on his way. He'll pick you up tomorrow, too. You'll work with him. I would appreciate it if you stayed away from me. It's the least you can do."

Shifting gears, she barely gave him time to shut the door and move back. She hit the gas, throwing pebbles and dirt into the air. A few might have pelted him, but he didn't notice.

He watched her drive away as he stood alone on a dark country road like an idiot. For most people, February 14 was Valentine's Day. But it was so much more for them.

When he finally worked up the nerve to ask her out as kids in school, Valentine's Day. Their first kiss, Valentine's Day. One year later, she'd lifted him out of darkness when she whispered she loved him. On Valentine's Day, their junior year, he'd asked if she'd be his and spend the rest of her life as his wife.

Despite her family's protests, she'd trusted him. She'd run away from everything she'd known to marry him in Vegas.

Now, he felt lost, trying to process the fact that one year after promising to love and cherish her, Danica had given birth to their babies. Alone.

Happy Valentine's Day.

The hole in his heart grew bigger. At this rate, the regrets of his life would fill all of Texas.

Chapter Five

"I can't believe he has the nerve to show up here." Jackie scooted closer to her on the pew. As always, they sat on the third bench. Her family never sat anywhere else, ever. Even on the rare occasion they were late, the pews were left open for them.

No need to look over her shoulder to see who her twin was horrified to see. Sweat beaded under her shirt. She resisted the urge to fan herself. What was he doing here?

"He's walking down the center aisle. Wait. He stopped. He's looking around." Jackie spoke the play-by-play through clenched teeth.

Danica stopped breathing for a moment. She frantically searched the sanctuary. The girls had left for children's church. Her father! Where was her father?

"Who's here?" Sammi sat on the opposite side. Her little sister didn't know what was going on. She twisted around.

Danica put her hand on her sister's leg. "Don't look back there."

Sammi gasped. "Is that—"

"Hush!" Head down, Danica relaxed her hands.

Her oldest sister, Nikki, moved into the pew in front of them with her husband, Adrian. With a narrowed gaze, her brother-in-law stared at them. "What's wrong?"

Sammi put her hand on the back of the board in front of her and leaned forward. "I might be imaging things, but I think that's Reid McAllister." She turned to Danica. "That's him, right? Did you know he was in town?"

Nikki's gaze darted between them and

Reid in the back of the church. Confusion seeped into her older sister's expression. "The father of the twins?" Nikki hadn't been around when Reid came home with her from college, so she didn't understand the history like her other sisters did.

As one, her family turned around. Her stupid heart missed a beat when she saw him standing alone. He had the look of a trapped animal, not knowing whether to run or fight. He had his black cowboy hat in front of him, the brim crushed in his grip.

On the other side of her, Jackie lowered her head and leaned in closer. "Not only is he here in town, but he's working at Danica's animal rescue place."

"What!" Sammi's eyes went wide. People started staring at them.

Stiff, Danica faced forward. "Shh." This conversation needed to end.

Adrian shifted to get a better look at them and the back of the church. "Wait. The twins' father is in town working for you, and you haven't told anyone?" He looked back at Danica. "Is he here to cause trouble for the girls?"

Danica closed her eyes to stop the urge to seek Reid out. "No."

"He didn't even know about the girls until I messed up and took them out to the ranch without talking to Danica. He saw them."

Adrian now looked as confused as Nikki, and a little angry. "You never told him you were pregnant?"

Jackie gave him a hard look and put her hand on Danica's shoulder. "He left her before she even knew. He just showed up and told her he's been in prison."

"What!" Sammi sat straight up.

"Shh." This time, they all shushed her. People filing into the church looked over at them.

Her family looked at her with different levels of shock, except for Jackie.

Her twin had gone back to glaring at Reid. Danica wanted to hide under the pew. "Can we not talk about this right now? The girls don't know, and I would prefer it if no one else knew until I figure out what to do."

"What about Daddy? He's going to have a fit if he sees Reid. That man doesn't have any right to be here. He needs to leave now." Jackie shot a hot glare to the back.

"You can't kick him out of a church. This is God's house. He has every right to be here." Danica didn't want to have any soft feelings for him, but if he really found God in prison, it wasn't for her to judge where he worshipped.

Two of her sisters were about to give their opinion when Mia, Adrian's daughter, joined them. She hugged her father's neck.

Danica touched Mia's arm. "Hey, sweetheart. Do me a big favor and find the twins. Just take them straight to children's church. Okay? After service, we'll all go to The Drug Store for lunch."

Mia stood and looked at them. Flipping

her braid back over her shoulder, she nodded. "Sure. Is everything okay?"

Adrian smiled and nodded. "Yeah. We just need to make sure the girls stay out of the sanctuary right now. I'll explain later."

With a quick kiss, she was gone.

Gripping her Bible, Danica kept her head down. "There's no way to keep Daddy out of here." She was going to be sick.

"This is ridiculous." Jackie put a hand on Danica's knee. "I'm going to tell him to move on down the road. There are like eight churches in this tiny town. He can go find God in one of those."

"Please don't. A scene at church is the last thing I need."

Jackie shook her head. "And you think when Daddy walks in here and sees him, there's not going to be fireworks?"

Nikki stood. "I'm going to talk to our church visitor and make sure he understands what's what." Without waiting for permission, she stood and marched straight down the aisle. Her military training radiated from every movement.

Adrian got up to follow. "Don't worry, I'll make sure she behaves." He patted Danica's hand, which now had a death grip on the back of the pew.

She forced herself to relax. If she didn't turn it into a big deal, then no one would even notice.

The youngest Bergmann sister sat back and crossed her arms. "Were you even going to tell me?"

Danica focused on the painting behind the baptismal. The mural of a tranquil Frio River stared back at her, painted by her grandmother five decades ago. Gram was gone now, but the love she had for her family and community lingered. What would she tell her to do?

Sammi turned again to watch the drama unfold behind them. She pressed her shoulder against Danica's as she whispered, "Pastor Levi is taking Reid to meet Lorrie Ann and Maggie."

Danica tried to tilt her head enough so she could see without being noticed. Nikki and Adrian arrived just as Reid shook hands with the pastor's wife and her aunt.

Maybe she should leave. The urge to run and hide battled with her need to stay and make sure her sisters didn't cause more problems. Her two worlds were colliding, and there was nothing she could do to stop the explosion. The best she could pray for was the least amount of damage, mainly to her daughters.

The pressure pushed against her temples. Not able to take it anymore, she stood. She needed to find her father before he joined the fun.

In the back room, she found her father with Sonia. Again. Her dad was spending a great deal of time with Lorrie Ann's mother.

When had her father start helping the choir get ready for worship?

"Daddy, I'm going to help with the children's church today." It wasn't unusual for her to volunteer, so her father didn't give her a second glance.

"Okay, sweetheart." He gave her a quick smile before going back to his task.

Sonia placed a hand on her father's arm and frowned at her. "Are you all right, Danica?" The woman was giving off a girlfriend vibe her sisters talked about, but she didn't have the time or energy to worry about her father's love life.

Straightening her back, she gave her a big smile. "It's all great."

Her father looked up, his gaze darting between the women. "Is there a problem?"

"No, Daddy. I'll see you after the service."

Once outside, she rested against the stone wall. Fresh air was good. She would need to let her father know Reid was in the area. This would be easier if Reid just stayed on the ranch.

Oh, no. The Hausman ranch brought the

steers in for the 4-H play-day each week-end. Her girls ran the barrels and poles. Her father had just gotten them a new horse to run. He was never going to miss this local event. What if Reid showed up, too?

"Danica?"

The rich, smooth drawl washed over her. His voice always melted her. Dropping her head, she closed her eyes. At least her father wouldn't see him if Reid was out here instead of inside the church.

"What are you doing here, Reid?" She opened her eyes and shifted her weight as her heels started sinking into the soft ground.

He looked good. His jawline smooth from a fresh shave, his jeans crisp and clean. A buttoned-up shirt starched under his black vest. Even his boots were free of dirt and grime. He didn't fit her image of a man who'd served time in prison.

As the bell started ringing, his gaze went from the town's main street to the church tower. After a long heavy pause, he took a breath but still didn't make eye contact. "I'm not following you. John Levi is one of the pastors with the prison ministry network. When he heard I was in the area, he came to visit and invited me to attend. I didn't know your family was here."

"Now you know."

He finally looked at her. The heat and accusation in his gray eyes forced her to look away. She had no reason to feel guilty.

"I can't sleep. Questions keep bouncing around in my head since I saw them. How were they as babies? When did they learn to walk? What were their first words? Who would it hurt for me to see them?" He stepped closer. "I also try and imagine you waddling in the last months, not able to get up. Did you have morning sickness the whole nine months?"

"Eight. It was eight months. They were early. I had to go home before they were released. Leaving the hospital without them was one of the worst days of my life."

He reached for her. His fingers brushing her shoulder before she stepped away.

"Don't. Touch. Me."

Thrusting his hands into his pockets, Reid put distance between them.

Breathing became easier, but each inhale brought a scent of fresh, clean soap. Danica wanted to lean into his neck and breathe deep. She pressed her back against the rough rock. It anchored her and kept her from doing something stupid. "It would be best if you left."

"I don't know if I can."

"There's nothing you can do." She glanced at him, then quickly looked away. The warm gray in his eyes mirrored the pain in her heart.

"Pastor Levi gave me a personal invitation to attend this church. The church where you and the girls worship. Don't you think God had something to do with that? Maybe I'm not supposed to walk away."

Blood slammed into her heart. "No. No, God has nothing to do with this." She needed him to go. The emotional roller coaster was wearing her down. She needed to get off. She didn't have time for this drama. To many people and animals were counting on her. The sanctuary needed her to stay focused. "Stay away from town. I'll get a restraining order."

With a couple of steps, he stood in front of her, forcing her to make eye contact. "Danica, calm down. I'm not going to hurt you or the girls." He rolled his shoulders. With his head back, he closed his eyes. "I just want… I'm not sure what I want, but I'll play by your rules. You're in charge. I just want the opportunity to see them. I asked Officer Bolton for the name of a family lawyer in Uvalde."

He brought his chin down, and his gaze penetrated her, holding her in place. "I want to give you the divorce, but I also want to know my rights as their father."

"You told James?" Breaking eye contact, she moved to the left. She started pacing, crushing acorns with each step.

"No. I just asked about a family lawyer."

She opened her mouth to speak a couple of times, but words became elusive. Feet planted, she forced herself to stop and look at him. "A divorce would be good. I also—"

The door in the hallway connected to the Sunday school classes opened. Amy, one of the children's church volunteers, poked her head out. "There you are. I'm glad I saw you out here. Suzie is sick."

"What's wrong? Where is she?" Danica rushed to Amy.

"In the bathroom with Mrs. Trees. She was singing, then suddenly she got sick."

"Where's Liz?" Danica followed Amy, then realized Reid was right on her heels. With a glare, she tried to tell him to back off, but he didn't seem to notice.

"Lizzy is in the craft room and happy as a lark. Do you want me to get her?"

"No. I'll take Suzie home. Will you tell my dad? Oh, wait. We came with him today…"

"I'll drive you home." Reid stood right behind her.

Her initial protest dropped away when she saw Suzie, flushed and sweaty.

Mrs. Trees held her, stroking her hair back. "Poor pumpkin. It just hit her so fast."

Danica took the youngest twin. Amy smiled. "I'll go tell your dad. Mr.…." She looked at Reid with a smile and raised an eyebrow.

He held out his hand. "Rei—"

Danica cut him off. "Tell Daddy that one of the guys from the wildlife sanctuary is taking us home." The girl nodded. "Thank you, Amy. You, too, Mrs. Trees."

"No worries. Hope she feels well soon."

Reid held the door open. "I'm parked behind this building. Do you want me to carry her?"

"Mommy, my tummy hurts."

She kissed Suzie's forehead. Heat radiated from her skin. "No, I have her. I'll just follow you. Honey, how are you feeling? Mr. McAllister is going to drive us home. Okay?"

Wrapping one arm around Danica's neck, her daughter rubbed her eyes and peeked at the man walking next to them.

Once they reached the ranch truck, she settled Suzie in the back and climbed in next to her. The diesel roared to life. Reid carefully made his way out of the church parking lot and onto the main road. How had she ended up in a truck with her husband?

Reid kept glancing at his passengers in the back seat. Danica gave him the directions to her home. One of his daughters was close to him. He wanted to talk to her, but…

He gripped the steering wheel and made sure to stay on the smoothest part of the country road. This opportunity might not happen again.

Checking on them in the rearview mirror, he saw Suzie's head in her mother's lap, Danica's long graceful fingers stroking her dark red curls.

"You sure have beautiful hair. Red is my favorite color."

"Thank you. My mommy and aunt Jackie have red hair, too, but theirs is lighter."

"My father had red hair the same as yours."

"Reid." Her voice drew deep with a warning.

"But you're—"

"Suzie!" Danica cut her off.

He pressed on. "My mother was Creole from New Orleans. My father was a red-headed Scotsman. Had the temper to go with it. You and your mom seem to be all sweet and not much spice."

She giggled. His heart melted. "My mom can get real mad, but not much. She gets mad when people hurt her animals."

"I imagine she'd get angry if someone hurt you, too."

Her little face was serious as she nodded. "On the bus, a boy put Lizzy's Hula-Hoop around her neck and left a bruise. When we got off the bus, Momma saw it right away and wanted to know who did it. She was so mad she chased down the bus and made it stop and charged inside. She made Shane apologize and got him suspended from school, and he still can't ride the bus. Boy, she was mad."

"Is Lizzy okay?" He met her eyes in the mirror. With a nod, she looked back down at the sick child leaning on her.

The gate to her family house appeared. As he eased down the drive to the two-story farmhouse, he had a strong sense of coming home, but it wasn't his home. He would never be part of this family. Knowing his girls had this, strong roots buried in love and faith, somewhat eased the pain. If he did nothing else right, at least his children had a mother who loved them and protected them from the ugliness of the world.

Reid parked and got out as Suzie started groaning again. "Momma, my tummy hurts real bad."

"Shh, it's okay, sweetheart. We're home." A gagging sound was the only warning before Suzie lost the rest of her stomach.

Reid opened the passenger door and released Suzie's seat belt. "I've got her. There's a blanket in the front you can use to wipe off. If you can unlock the door, I'll take her to the bathroom. You can change."

"Mommy, I'm sorry." Her daughter started sobbing.

"Shh." Reid gently moved her away from the mess. "Moms are…um, waterproof. We'll just take her out back and wash her off." He lifted the five-year-old as if she weighed nothing. And he didn't even hesitate over the mess. "Thankfully, most landed on the truck floor, so we're all good."

With the blanket, she cleaned it off. "Reid, go to the side door. It's open."

With their daughter pulled up against his chest, he turned to the left with a scowl. "Does it stay unlocked with you and the girls inside, too?"

She tried not to be insulted by the tone of his voice. "It's Clear Water. Nothing ever happens here."

That wasn't completely true. The father of her children was in her house, helping her with a sick child. She had a feeling there would be no going back from here.

Leaning down while keeping Suzie close, he pushed open the kitchen door. Their daughter had her arms wrapped around his neck as he walked into her home.

Pulling her jacket off, Danica threw it over the bench. Her shoes were next. It would be easier to throw the whole outfit away.

Her shoulders had a new weight on them, and it had nothing to do with a sick daughter. Her phone vibrated in the jacket pocket.

Careful not to touch anything gross, she checked the number. It seemed all her sisters suddenly needed to talk to her.

Tossing the phone on the table, she headed to the washroom. She had a load of clean clothes in the dryer. "Take her to her room. It's the third door on the right from the stairs. I'll be right there."

She hurried into clean clothes and left everything on the floor. She'd get it later.

Rushing up the stairs, she froze at the girls' bedroom door. The man she had given everything to in another lifetime sat on the edge of the narrow pink bed covered with stuffed animals. Curled up with her head resting on his thigh, Suzie was asleep. She was already cleaned up and settled.

He was staring at their daughter. Raising his head, he looked at Danica. Awe and terror seemed to be swirling in those moss green eyes.

Clearing his throat, his focus returned to the sleeping child. "She got her favorite nightgown, and I got a washcloth from the bathroom." Running the cloth across her forehead with one hand, Reid rested the other on her shoulder. "She's so small."

She needed to get him out of here before her heart completely melted or her family showed up. "Thank you. I've got it now. I'm sorry about the truck. I can—"

"Don't worry about it. It's made for handling mud, and anything else you get from working on a ranch with animals. Are you all right?"

She chuckled, remembering his words. "Yeah. You know us moms. Wash-and-wear." Moving to the bed, she took the washcloth from him. "You need to go. I have a feeling the family will be here soon, and it'll be easier if you're not here."

"Right." Keeping his gaze on Suzie, he gently lifted her head and put her back on her pillow. "She seems better. Just tired now." He looked up at her. "Are you taking her to the doctor?"

"If she is still sick tomorrow, I will." She eased onto the bed, taking the place where he had been sitting. "Bye, Reid."

He nodded. "If she needs anything else, you'll let me know?"

"My dad and sisters will be here soon. We've got this covered."

He took his hat off and backed out of the girls' room. His gaze lingered on the walls. Walls covered with posters of horses, family pictures and…

Oh, no. The painting. She could tell the minute Reid saw it.

"Danica. That's the drawing I did for you." It was a whimsical ink drawing of a garden with baby animals having a tea party under giant sunflowers. Washes of color danced across the picture. He had made the frame from scraps of old wood that he'd found in one of their barns.

It had been his Valentine's gift to her the day he asked her to marry him. He'd told her they would create their own world. She gritted her teeth.

"Reid. It doesn't mean anything. I never told them who painted it. I always loved your art, and it's perfect for the girls' room." She brushed back her daughter's hair. "You need to go."

He turned at the door and paused, hand on the frame. "The Hausmans said they're providing steers for the county play-day next weekend. Do the girls ride there?"

"They run the barrels and poles." She needed to stop talking. "If you see us there, you can say hi." Her sisters were going to kill her. Now she had to warn her father. "I'll tell Daddy you're in town." She looked down to make sure Suzie was still asleep. "I want to make it clear, this is not me giving you permission to tell them who you are. You said you just wanted to see them. That's all this is."

"I get it. Thank you." With a nod, he left.

She went back to tending to their daughter. Her daughter. He would be gone as soon as she had a new vet tech. The idea of him leaving should not make her sad.

Gritting her teeth, she reminded herself why loving him again was a mistake. She had already grieved the lost dreams of them growing old together, raising their family. Enough time was wasted over Reid McAllister. She couldn't afford to give him any more of her.

Chapter Six

"Daddy, please. Don't cause any trouble." Danica gripped the railing on the stock trailer and peered through the bars at her father. He eased the big palomino gelding out the back.

"I'm not the one you need to worry about." He glanced around the area behind the arena. "Where are the girls?"

"They went to the concession stand with Nikki and Mia."

"You think that's wise? What if he sees them and does something?"

"Like what?" Hands on her hips, she stared

at him. "He's not going to do anything other than say hi. We have an agreement."

"I suppose you trust him? Just like the last time." He looped the lead rope and checked the saddle. "I think we should get the girls and go home."

She tried to imagine how he would react if she told him that they were married. A shudder skipped up and down her spine. No way did she want to face that disappointment. Okay, it was official. She was a coward. "No. They wouldn't understand, and they would be devastated. They don't know who he is other than he works with me at the sanctuary."

He shook his head as he went back into the trailer to get the pony, Cinnamon. "You and your lost causes. I don't understand." He stopped and looked at her through the slots. "Most kidnappings are done by a biological parent."

She closed her eyes and took a deep breath. "Daddy, he's not going to kidnap them."

"He's already been in prison once. What's going to stop him from taking them and skipping town?"

"I think he's trying to make things right. He wants to see them. That's all. They are his daughters." Her stomach plunged downward. They were his daughters, and nothing would change that.

"You don't think it's a bit strange that of all the places he could have moved to, he ended up in your backyard? Working on your sanctuary."

"He thinks God put him here." She didn't know what to believe.

Her father snorted. "God has nothing to do with him."

"Daddy, you don't know that."

"I know he hurt my little girl. He walked out on you. And if he tries anything with my granddaughters…"

Placing a hand on his shoulder, she tried to think of words that would make him understand the position she was in. "Daddy, he's the reason you have these granddaughters. They are as much his as they are mine." When did she get in the business of defending Reid?

"He's already working his way back into your life. I'm not going to pick up the pieces again. If he says more than hi to the twins, I'm calling James."

"I can give you his number if you need it." Reid stood at the edge of the old green Suburban, a bottle of Big Red soda in his hand. "My parole officer is here tonight, so if you feel the need to talk to him about me, go ahead."

Her father didn't say a word, but if looks could kill, she'd be writing Reid's obituary. She stepped between the men. "Hi, Reid."

"I saw the girls at the concession stand. Figured you'd want to be around when I talked to them." He turned to her father, head down. With a deep breath, he stood straighter and looked her father in the eye. "Mr. Bergmann, I know you have every reason to hate me and rightly so, but I want you to know that I'm not here to hurt Danica or the girls in any way. I do have amends to make, and I hope you believe me when I say that I am truly sorry."

"It's God's place to forgive you, not mine. And keep those sunglasses on. Otherwise, people will start asking questions about your eye color." With the lead in hand, her father took the pony to the other side of the trailer.

"Reid, I'm sorry."

"Don't be. He's right." He turned his face to the opposite side of the arena. "I saw them with Frito pies and Big Red."

She checked Jingle's hooves. "Big Red is their favorite. We don't have soda in the house, so it's a special treat once a week." Moving to the gelding's mane, she started braiding it. His neck was chest level to her.

After a moment of silence, she stopped and looked at him over the pony. She probably shouldn't tell him this, but her mouth opened and… "Every time they get one, I think about you and your obsession with the drink. Strange, the things they inherit."

"Do they like school?"

"They're only in kindergarten. But they love school. They ask tons of questions and enjoy talking and being around people. Animals, too. They're obsessed with animals, all kinds, even insects. The other day they found a spider in the house. Sammi was going to kill it, but they made my dad catch it and release it outside."

He smiled at her, and his eyes sparkled. That's the expression she lost her heart to, the same expression she had seen in her daughters. Turning away from him, she tried to think of something else to say.

The girls were dangerous to talk about. They were her weak spot. "How's your mother doing? It had to be hard on her when you went to prison." She needed to remind them both why he didn't know his children. It was the consequence of his mistakes, his choices.

He'd always been worried about his mom, but Danica never got to meet her. She never thought about her as her children's grandmother. She hadn't even thought about his side of the family at all.

His hands in his pockets, Reid's gaze locked on to some far-off place. Someplace she couldn't see. "Reid?"

"Mom died my second year in." His jaw popped.

The world went quiet as she focused on him. She stepped around the horse she had put between them, wanting to be closer. Wanting to wrap him in her arms. "Reid…" She stepped forward.

Reid looked at Danica as she moved toward him, but the sound of sweet giggles stole his attention away. The twins, his daughters, were running toward him. One of them had on a pink cowboy hat with matching boots and a glittering shirt. The other one wore a black hat to go with her dark purple bandana. They had cheesy Frito pies in hand, and their aunt Jackie carried a couple bottles of the cold drink he loved.

"Mr. Reid!"

"Hello."

The girls greeted him with a smile. Standing behind them, Jackie glared. Her thoughts on him being here had been made perfectly clear.

A huge silver dually with a matching horse trailer pulled up behind them. With the engine cut off, Nikki jumped down from the passenger side, followed by her stepdaughter, Mia. The frown on her face made it clear he was not welcomed. "Oh, look, the whole family is here."

Danica put her hand on Suzie's shoulder. "Nikki."

With a shake of her head, the oldest Bergmann sister scanned the area. "Where's Sammi?"

Mr. Bergmann came from the other side of the trailer and shook Adrian's hand. "Her horse was hyped up, so she's running off his energy in the arena. Need any help unloading?"

Suzie shoved the last spoonful of chili into her mouth. "Can I go? I want to warm up Sunny."

Lizzy shook her head. "Nothing is going to make him go faster."

Suzie started arguing.

"Girls, stop it." Jackie held up the bottles. "Do you want the rest of your soda?"

"Can you put it in the ice chest, please?" Suzie glared at her sister. "I want to save it for later."

She moved to the palomino tied at the end of the trailer. Standing next to the big gelding, his daughter looked so small. Reid laid a hand on the thick neck. "This is your horse?"

Suzie nodded. "I wanted a faster horse, but Grandpa says I have to wait until I'm double digits. That's a long time. Momma, can I ride now?"

"Be careful and stay on the railing."

She unfastened the reins and looked at him. "Can you help me mount? I just need you to cup your hands so I can reach the stirrup."

He steadied his breath. It didn't mean anything. He was just the closest to Suzie and her horse.

Lizzy sat on the side step of the trailer, her Frito pie in her lap and her Big Red next to her. "If you rode a smaller horse, you could mount yourself."

"I don't want a baby's horse."

"Jingles is not for babies. He runs. He runs faster than Sunny. All he does is trot."

"Yeah, but Jingles's legs are so short he has a slower time."

"Girls, stop it, or we can load the horses up and go home."

"Yes, ma'am," both girls mumbled.

Reid smiled as Suzie put her pink-booted foot in his cupped hands. With ease, she leaped into the saddle and adjusted the reins as she slipped the tip of her toes into the stirrups, heels down. She sat well in the saddle.

"Mr. Reid, do you ride?"

"I do. I rope, and I've been known to ride a bull or two."

Danica smiled. "The first time I saw him, he was riding a bull."

Lizzy's eyes went wide. "The first time? Where was that?"

Reid looked at Danica, wondering if she'd meant to say something about their past. By the stiffness in her shoulders and slight panic and regret in her gaze, he assumed not.

Mr. Bergmann reappeared then, his long strides bringing him next to Lizzy. Quickly, he lifted her up over his head, causing her to giggle. He pressed his nose to hers. "Are we going to ride today or just sit around and talk?" The girls forgot their questions and cheered. Back on the ground, Lizzy mounted the shorter horse.

Suzie pulled back on her reins and moved

the big gelding away from the trailer. "I'm going to be out there before you."

"Girls, it's not a race." They ignored their mother.

With a kick to her horse, Suzie moved out into a trot. Her red hair bounced around her shoulders. "I'm going to beat you!" she yelled at her sister as Lizzy mounted her pony.

Danica stood with her hands on her hips. "Careful, girls, or the horses are going back into the trailer."

Mia moved her horse past them. "I'll watch them."

Mr. Bergmann followed the three girls to the arena.

Danica turned away from Reid. "I can't believe I said that. Why did I tell them I knew you before? Where was my brain?" She slammed a few straps of leather into a bag.

Danica frantically moved around, stuffing things in a large black bag. She was mad at herself. Off to the side, Reid looked like he wanted to say something.

Jackie acted first, slamming the lid to the big silver ice chest. Standing, she crossed her arms and glared at Reid. "Since they were born, everyone makes comments about their eye color. Even to this day, when I take them somewhere, it is the first thing people see. If you're serious about respecting Danica, and not forcing the issue, then you need to stay out of town and away from people that know the girls."

Danica's face tightened. She shut the back door of the Suburban and just stood there, looking at nothing. "Maybe it would be eas-ier if I just told the girls."

"No." Reid and Jackie stared at each other, startled to find themselves in agreement.

He cleared his throat. "They would want to know where I've been. I can't lie to them. I can't tell them the truth, either."

"So it's about you being embarrassed." Jackie leaned back against the trailer. "What about you just disappearing again? You've been here for a little over two weeks. Danica's a grown woman and can make her own mistakes, but my nieces have big hearts. They haven't learned to protect them yet. I'm not going to let you crush them just so you can play daddy for a little bit."

"Enough." Danica pushed her way between Reid and her sister. "I agree. The girls aren't ready." Her gaze jumped between the two of them. "For all the reasons you stated, and more. Jackie, I love you, but this isn't your fight."

"You're thinking of taking him back, aren't you? How can you still love him? After everything he did?"

"I don't love him." On the edge of yelling, she closed her eyes and swallowed.

She didn't love him anymore. He knew that, but it still hurt to hear the words.

"This isn't about me. I have to figure out what is best for Suzie and Lizzy. If you'll excuse me, I'm here to watch my daughters ride." Green eyes stared him down. "You have steers to take care of."

She hoped the message was clear. *Don't join the family.* He gave her a quick nod. "I'll see you Monday at the sanctuary."

Danica took her sister's hand and headed to the arena.

After a few riders, the announcer called Suzie as the next rider. Reid went to the railing and pulled himself up to get a better look. He scanned the stands. Right up front, Danica sat with her father and two of her sisters. They were laughing about something.

Ready to take pictures, Mr. Bergmann had a camera with a monster zoom lens. Reid wished he had something to take a picture with, but his phone was so basic it wouldn't be able to take one from this far.

Adrian joined him. They stood there in silence, but for some reason, he didn't feel as alone as he had before. The big gelding moved to the gate. With a kick, Suzie leaned forward and urged her horse to move through the clover pattern.

He had to smile. The big animal flicked his ears back and forth but never went past a trot.

Adrian laughed. "That girl would give anything for a faster horse. They're having a hard time keeping her on that pace. She wants speed."

"What about Lizzy?"

"Oh, she's the slow, steady one. She's happy with the pony. I don't see her advancing to the upper-level rodeos. She's just here for the Frito pie and Big Red."

"Hey, Reid!" James hollered.

He jumped at his parole officer's voice. For a moment, he panicked wondering what he'd done wrong. "Have you seen Danica? We have a problem. It seems a few of the big cats got through the fencing on the west side and were seen stalking goats."

"There's no way they got out."

"All I know is we got a few angry ranchers

at the sanctuary, demanding something be done. Or they're going to start taking care of the situation themselves."

He glanced across the arena and found Danica looking at him. She turned away when they made eye contact. "I'll go get her. Let me tell Philip I'm leaving, and make sure he can get the steers back to the Hausman ranch without me."

"I can help him if he needs it," Adrian offered. "She'll need backup with those ranchers. They've been looking for ways to shut her down from day one."

Reid nodded and made his way to Danica. Taking the stairs two at a time, he ignored Jackie's hard glare at the landing and went straight to Danica. "Hey. There's trouble at the sanctuary."

Chapter Seven

Parking behind Stephanie's Mercedes, Danica got out of her vehicle and slammed the door behind her, striding toward the oncoming storm.

Reid followed her. On the porch, a group of men in cowboy hats, starched jeans and worn boots gathered around Officer Bolton and the lawyer.

A barrel-chested rancher, Walter Riggs, stepped away from the group when he saw them. "You promised us they wouldn't be a threat to our herds."

Marching up the steps, Danica faced him

directly. "Y'all are a bigger threat to my old crippled cats than they are to your stock."

That was the wrong thing to say. A flurry of angry words flew through the air.

Reid took a step forward but stopped right behind her left shoulder. "Yelling at her won't fix the problem."

She'd lost her composure for a moment. That couldn't happen again. They were threatening her animals, and she needed to keep a level head in order to protect them. Reid stared straight at the lead cowboy.

Reid stood tall but relaxed. "We'll collect the cats, fix the fences and put procedures in place to make sure this doesn't happen again." He glanced down at Danica.

She nodded, grateful he had a cool head. With the aviators on, he was an imposing figure.

His finger brushed her back, but he quickly retreated and crossed his arms over his chest.

With a clear focus, she took control of

the conversation. "It's our priority to discover how this happened, and make sure it doesn't happen again. For the safety of your livestock, and of the rescue animals on the premises."

Walter closed the space between them. With his hands on his hips, he lifted his chin in a challenge. "Who are you?"

"I'm her vet tech, and I just got out of prison, so I don't scare easily."

Her father's friend took a step back. He glanced to the deputy, then back to Reid. "Is that a threat?"

"No, sir. Just letting you know you can't come here expecting to bully Ms. Bergmann. Her family wouldn't appreciate it."

"Reid." Her hand touched his arm. The warmth seeped through the cotton material of his shirt, so she pulled her hand away quickly. "Reid, as he said, is my vet tech. He's worked with large animals before. We will have the cats back on the property before nightfall."

Another long, lanky rancher spoke up. "We don't have a problem with you or your animals if they stay on your place. Danica, you promised these cats wouldn't be a threat to our livestock. Now they are running wild over the countryside. I have my boys out looking for them. We're going to get them off our ranch one way or another." He shot a nervous glance at Reid. "If you get them first, that's fine, but I'm not sure this is the place for this kind of rescue facility. It's surrounded by working ranches."

James stepped up. "Now, there's no reason for threats, Henry."

Stephanie straightened her jacket. "We have every legal right to be here. If you have any complaints, make them formal. Showing up at the sanctuary as a mob is not acceptable." She glanced at her phone. "I've got an appointment, but if you need anything else, you know how to contact me."

"Thank you, Stephanie." Danica turned to Reid. "I'm going to move the car. Can you gather the supplies we need for retrieval, and bring the truck and stock trailer around?"

Without taking his eyes off the small group of men, he nodded. She didn't want to think how easy it was to trust him, especially in a tense situation like this. No, for now, she needed to focus on the real problem. She needed to get her cats home.

"The crippled jaguar is close to the fence line, hiding under a cedar. He's acting like he wants back in the sanctuary. I've got a small team here, including James." Bobby's thick drawl came over the radio. Reid looked over at Danica as she listened in.

"We have the small female. Reid and I are taking her back, and we'll put her in the clinic for tonight. Did James get pictures of the fences?"

"Yes, ma'am. Looks like someone cut the fence, then chased the cats out."

"Can you make the opening bigger, then try to herd the jag in that direction? If we can get him back without tranquilizing him that would be great."

"With the volunteers, we can also secure the fence in no time. We'll have it back right as rain before the sun sets."

"Thank you, Bobby."

"Sure thing." The line went dead.

Slamming a fist against the steering wheel, Danica's delicate jaw looked hard as steel. "This was done on purpose. Who would want to close us down so bad?"

"You'll need to make a list and turn it over to the sheriff. Hopefully, they'll take it seriously and investigate."

With a rigid jerk of her chin, she stayed focused on the road in front of her. They sat in silence until she parked behind the clinic. Even then, she only gave short, direct instructions to help her with the animal.

Checking the cat, they placed her in a holding crate. Danica briskly put things away, her movements stiff. She started wiping down an area she'd already hit twice before.

He moved behind her, and gently placed his hands on her upper arms to hold her still. "It's going to be okay." He pressed his face into her hair. For a moment, everything was right with the world. She was in his arms, her warmth and scent surrounding him.

She relaxed against him. The citrus smell of her shampoo flirted with his senses. Just as quickly, she braced her hand on the counter and stiffened. "Reid, you don't know that."

Turning to face him, she tried to put distance between them. If she wanted space, she wasn't getting it. He had her trapped against the counter. She needed to listen to him. "Dani girl, it's going to be okay."

With a grumble, she ducked under his arm and started to rearrange containers. "Go see Bobby."

"Baby. You're upset. I know I'm part of the problem, but you've been so strong for so long." Standing next to her, he placed a hand over hers to ease the nervous moments.

"If you're mad, get mad. I can take it, then you can go back to being strong."

Suddenly she was in his arms, her fist hitting his chest, her face on his shoulder. Feet planted, he took the hits with his arms around her.

"I'm tired of being the strong one. I'm tired of being responsible for everyone and everything else! You left me. You left me to take care of everyone and I…" With a sob, she collapsed against him.

Digging his fingers into her hair, he held her close as tears saturated his shirt. His own might have joined hers. "I'm sorry. I'm so sorry." He repeated the useless phrase over and over against the soft skin of her ear.

Taking two hard gasping breaths, she lifted her head. Her green eyes were bright with tears. "Why? Why did you throw us away for a quick score?"

A question that had tormented him for the last few years. There was never an answer good enough. "I lacked faith."

His thumb traced her bottom lip. He became fixated as memories of their first kiss rose to the forefront. She had been so sweet and tender on that cold February day. She was stronger now.

Dropping his hands, he leaned in closer. Closer to the dream that had sustained him for the last six years. Closer to the peace she always gave him.

Soft as he remembered, her lips gave way under his. He went deeper. His hand cupped her jaw as he explored and rediscovered the wonder of Danica, his wife.

One step closer. He had waited for this for a lifetime. Time stood still as he claimed what had once been his.

Danica pushed on his chest. "No." One step and she was beyond his reach again.

Yanked out of his dreams, he faced the cold, hard reality of his choices. He let her go.

Moving to the other side of the room, the heated glare she shot at him made her mood clear. With the medical table between them, she brought her breathing back under control. "No. Not now. Not ever again." Spinning around, she rubbed her face. "I had my meltdown. You need to go now. Bobby will be back soon, and he can take you to the ranch."

"Danica, I'm sorry." He had to find a way to reach her.

"Yeah, I heard you the first few hundred times. I forgive you. We're done." Dry-faced, she stiffened her spine and looked at him straight in the face. "I know you're invited to our church. If you do attend, please don't talk to the girls or me. I recommend that you stay away from everyone in my family."

"If I were a better man, I would without question. But I can't ignore the part of me that wants to fight for my family. For my rights as a father."

The color drained from her face. "Please don't. You've hurt us enough. The best thing would be for you to go. Leave before the girls learn who you are and what you've done."

"Would that be so bad?"

"I would rather they not learn that their father transported drugs. That he comes from a line of people who took the easy path to prison. You're not the kind of man I want in their lives."

Every doubt he had walloped him in the face. He grabbed the edge of the counter for support. His girls would be ashamed of him. Just as their mother was. He was the son of Calvin McAllister, and he was drenched in the sins of his father. His insides hollowed out, not an ounce of blood or a twitch of muscle was evident. It was gone. Ray had promised him God's forgiveness if he asked for it. Forgiveness from Danica was not so easy. "I don't even deserve it."

Eyes narrowed, she glared at him. "What are you talking about?"

"Forgiveness. I know it doesn't erase my

mistakes." His jaw hurt. "I don't deserve you or the girls. Knowing I haven't earned the right to have you in my life doesn't stop the wanting. I want to be in the girls' lives in some sort of way."

A few labeled containers seemed to be out of place as she turned her back to him and rearranged them again.

He straightened. "I'll check the cub." He glanced at the large crate that held the still-sleeping female cat. "Do you need help releasing her?"

He waited at the door for her to say something. What he wanted, he wasn't sure, but he didn't want to leave her this way. Her back stayed rigid, and her usually graceful moments were stiff. She dropped a canister of swabs, and they scattered across the cold tiled floor.

He rushed to help her.

"Reid, just go. I can—"

"Momma!"

"Momma, can we see the baby bats?"

Her head dropped, but only for a brief second. Steel in her eyes, she glared at him. "Go."

"Mr. McAllister!"

"Call me Reid." He smiled at them as he went down to their eye level. "Mr. McAllister makes me look around for my father."

The twins giggled. Their aunt Jackie walked up behind them, placing her hands on their shoulders. She encircled them and pulled them back a little.

"Mr. Reid, have you seen the baby bats?"

He rotated to face them. "Yep. Yesterday I fed them and gave them their bath."

They clapped and jumped. "We got to watch Momma bathe them, but we're not allowed to play with them. They like us, though."

"They're the cutest things ever!" They both turned to their mom. Identical moss gray eyes, full of wonder and all the good things in life, took his breath away. He never knew such beautiful parts of him could ever exist on God's earth.

"Can we see the baby bats now? We won't touch them."

"No, sweethearts. They need to be free of human contact as much as possible."

Their sweet faces fell, and he wanted their smiles back. "I took a little video of them yesterday." He pulled his phone from his back pocket. "Do you want to see it?"

"Yes!" The girls echoed in stereo as they ran to him.

"Girls!" Their mother and aunt had the same stereo effect. He couldn't help but smile.

"Reid." Danica joined them, putting both of her hands on Suzie. "You can't—"

"It's just a video."

"We want to see it," the girls said in unison.

He hit Play and held his phone out so the girls could see the small screen. They stood in awe, giggling and squealing each time the bats moved. He forced a smile. The longing to pull them close and take in everything about them dumbfounded him. It hurt deep in his gut.

"Okay, girls." Danica's tone remained firm, the voice of a protective mother. "That's enough. I need to feed the cub. Want to go with me?"

"But we want to watch it again!"

"No, we need to let Mr. McAllister get back to work." Jumping, they went to her. It didn't take long to lose their attention. "Come on. We need to get the formula." She took their hands in each of hers.

For a moment, he imagined them parenting together. She would be fussing at him for never telling the girls no. "I can text the video to you."

The girls cheered. Jackie rolled her eyes. "Send it to me. Danica has a lousy phone. You know, since she has to support her family on her own."

"Jackie!"

Ignoring her sister, Jackie gave him her number. "Come on, girls. Let's go."

Lizzy started following, but stopped and looked back at him. "Are you coming with us?"

His heart skipped. Danica started to speak only to be cut off by Jackie as she stepped in between them. "No, he has to stay here." Her glare made it clear he wasn't welcome.

Stepping to the side, Danica looked at him, her eyes a bit softer, but not much. "Mr. McAllister has work to do here."

He stood and put the phone back in his pocket. He had Jackie's number, not that it would do him any good, but it was a connection to his girls that he didn't have before.

Pausing at the door, Danica sent the girls ahead with Jackie. He held his breath, waiting to hear her voice. Anything to keep her in his physical world.

"Don't forget to record your time so I can sign it. It's due to Officer Bolton Monday, right?"

"Yes, ma'am." He stuffed his hands in his pockets.

With a nod, she left and jogged to catch up with Jackie and the twins. He moved to the door. A hollow feeling settled inside him as he watched his family walk away.

Once they were out of sight, he went to the supply room at the back of the building. His thoughts kept returning to the girls' faces as they watched his video. They had looked at him with such excitement and love.

In their life, they hadn't been taught to be wary and skeptical of strangers. They had a protected life. To them, the world was a good and safe place.

What would happen if they found out he was their father? He broke out into a cold sweat.

Stopping at the orphaned bats' station, he checked on them. Each was wrapped tightly in a little bright-colored towel. They were surprisingly cute. Big eyes and ears, tiny little noses, and completely dependent on the kindness of the humans in charge of them.

One of the little guys yawned and blinked at him a couple of times before snuggling back against his brother bat. Reid took out his phone and snapped a few pictures. The girls would love it.

With Jackie's number already memorized, he sent the pictures to her and hoped she would share them with Suzie and Lizzy.

Scanning the room, he noticed so many things. Old and broken-down. A forgotten forge. He figured most would find it a lost cause, but he saw potential. If he knew Danica, she thought the same thing.

A thought occurred to him, and he got an idea. The genuine smile felt good on his face. Doing a quick search on the internet through his phone, he smiled again. Live camera feed.

The girls might not be able to spend as much time with the baby bats as they wanted, but this way they could keep an eye on them and watch all the activities that helped the bats grow stronger.

Looking at his phone again, he reckoned he had enough time to plan another project that he'd been considering since the first time he drove the property with Danica.

Chapter Eight

Danica restocked the butterscotch candy on the counter. The free sweet was a tradition going back to when the first Bergmanns ran the lumberyard.

Growing up, she'd felt trapped by the old limestone walls. The fact her family had owned the building since the founding of Clear Water hadn't meant anything to her then. Now it gave her comfort and a place for her daughters to belong.

Even the family squabbles gave her a sense of comfort. At this moment, Jackie and her father were in the loft, debating a new arrangement of the store.

She chuckled at the predictability of her family.

The bell chimed, and she looked up to greet the customer. Her smile slipped.

Reid. If she didn't know better, she'd think he was tormenting her. All day she had fought to keep him out of her thoughts. She wasn't winning the battle.

He stood at the door, not moving forward.

Danica braced her hands on the edge of the counter. She was glad to have something between them. "What are you doing here, Reid?"

With a frown, he looked mad at her. "What are you doing here? Don't you work at the sanctuary during the day?"

"Not on Tuesdays and Wednesdays. I cover the—" Why was she explaining herself to him? "It's a family business. Family has to work it."

"Do the girls spend time here?" He walked

over to a poster and looked at the illustrations of the building from the day it was opened over one hundred years ago. Another picture was from two years ago, when it was added to the list of Texas Historical Buildings.

He bent to get a closer look. "There're the girls." With just the tip of his fingers, he touched the glass. "They've grown since this was taken. Do you have more pictures of them?"

"Why are you in the store?" Leaving the safety of the counter, she headed to the nail and screw aisle. She'd been sorting inventory when Jake came in for his supplies. "Did the ranch send you? They usually call in their orders ahead of time." It would be easier to talk to him if she was busy. Someone had mixed the nails. Her father would have a fit if he saw the mess.

"No. I came to talk to Adrian. I was told he'd be working here today. Upstairs."

"Oh." Why did it matter that he hadn't

come seeking her? "Yeah, he's with Nikki. I think they're taping and floating the new drywall. What do you need to talk to him for?"

"About a job." Head tilted back, Reid looked at the decorative tin that covered the tall ceiling.

"Already tired of wrangling for the Hausmans?" Okay, that sounded snarky. Without turning, she glanced at him from the corner of her eye.

Reid shook his head and crammed his hands deep into the front pockets of his jacket. Now he studied the old wooden floor. His profile was hard and impressive, even with uncertainty etched in every line.

"I like working with the horses. With you looking for a new vet tech, I thought I'd line up more work. Pastor Levi said Adrian might have something for me. I like staying busy. Keeps me out of trouble."

"It won't be that easy. My brother-in-law is one of the hardest-working guys I know.

He has a strong sense of commitment and loyalty. He doesn't like working with people who might just up and leave, abandoning a project."

"Ouch." No emotion went along with the word. His gaze stayed on the back of the store.

"Sorry. I just don't—"

"Baby, it's okay. Don't worry about it." At the counter, he picked up a flyer announcing the fund-raiser for the sanctuary.

She knew he used the term of endearment without thinking, but it still did things to her.

"Rodeo Bonanza? The guys were talking about this. You know I rode in prison. They held a first-class show." He looked at her with the smile of old on his face. "I was riding the first time we met. Right after being introduced to you, I was so distracted the bull tossed me at the gate."

She couldn't help but laugh at the memory. "You're still blaming that bad ride on me?" Walking to the end of the aisle, Danica crossed her arms and leaned on the endcap.

"You were the best thing that ever—"

"Mr. McAllister." Her father stomped down the stairs. "Can I help you?"

Glancing up, she found her sister on the edge of the railing, staring down at them from the loft. Her father directed a frown at Reid before he turned and made eye contact with Danica. Her twin shook her head as if disappointed.

Now what had she done? She scowled back and shrugged. As an adult woman, if she wanted to talk to the father of her children, it was not the place of her twin to judge.

"Sir, I came looking for Adrian. I was told he—"

"He's upstairs." Standing next to Danica now, her father waved to the stairs. "It's that way. Turn to the left. You can't miss him."

"Thank you, sir." With a respectful nod, Reid slowly took the stairs. Passing through the office loft, he greeted Jackie. She didn't say anything, but her gaze stayed on him as if waiting for a rattlesnake to strike.

Reid was a proud man. To keep smiling at their obvious hostility had to be a difficult hit to his pride.

The first time Danica brought him home to meet her father, it had not gone well. Despite his promise not to cause problems, the twenty-year-old Reid had not been able to ignore any slight that he saw as an insult to his manhood.

It had been a week of the two men arguing and stomping around each other like two bulls in a small pen. She had been so stressed, trying to keep the peace between them. By the end of the visit, she'd just wanted to get back to school.

Back to just the two of them. With Danica, Reid had been such a different person. When it had just been the two of them, she'd never seen the angry young man her father and sisters had.

That should have been a warning sign, but

the haze of love had been too thick for her to pay attention. The bitter truth was her father had been right.

"Danica!" Her father said it as if he'd already called her a few times.

"Sorry, Daddy. Did you need something?" She went back to organizing and counting nails.

"Do you still love him?" The deep lines of his face were not from smiling.

"Daddy." Head down, she recounted the box.

In silence, he stared at her for a bit.

She gave up on her task and looked at him with her hands on her hips. "No."

He raised one eyebrow.

Taking a deep breath, she stood still despite the urge to fidget with her shirt. It was not a lie. It wasn't. *Please, God, don't let it be a lie.*

"She's lying!" Jackie yelled from the loft, arms crossed.

"Am not." Great. They had dissolved into

five-year-olds. All she needed to do was stomp her foot.

"Whatever, but lying to yourself is not going to help anyone." Jackie turned and disappeared into the office. Fine, she'd let her sister have the last word this time.

Her father moved closer. "Be careful. You have the girls. Don't make the mistake I did. Being with the wrong person is not worth it. God has someone for you. A Godly man who will love you and the girls the way you deserve."

Since her jaw was locked, she just nodded. Reid might be as selfish as Sheila, Sammi's mother, but Danica was afraid it was already too late for her heart. Maybe she had never actually stopped loving Reid. She'd just buried it, waiting for him to come back.

"I promise, Daddy, my girls will always come first." They would not experience the pain that had left her heart a scarred, bloody mess. Her mom's death, her oldest sister's departure, running away, her stepmother not loving them enough to stay. And Reid.

But being tired of trying to stay strong was not an excuse. Danica could overcome any weakness that encouraged her to accept Reid as her one and only love. He'd already demonstrated he couldn't be trusted.

Just because he hadn't started an argument with her father or sister this one time didn't prove anything. Second chances were God's business, not hers.

Anger sat in his gut like embers. He needed to release the pent-up tension. There was nothing for him to prove. He hated the anger his father had planted in him.

It was up to him to not give in to it. Something physical always helped. Back at the ranch, the guys had a punching bag set up in one of the barns. He pressed his right thumb into his left palm.

"Reid?" Nikki stood in the doorway of the front room.

Remodeling a house was hard work, but it would keep him focused. Physical work, that's what he needed. He liked having a mission.

"Hi, Nikki." The oldest Bergmann had different coloring but still looked just like the twins. They seemed a lot like their father at first, but they looked more like their mother from the old photos Danica had shown him once. If he remembered correctly, they were about the same age now as their mother was when she died.

Adrian came up behind Nikki, resting a hand on her shoulder. "Hey, Reid. What's up?"

"Bobby's been doing little things around the house on the sanctuary, the one that has fire damage. At the rate it's going, it will take years. I told him that I could add it to my volunteer hours and we could get it done faster. I thought you might help me figure out some of the details. But I don't want

Danica and the girls to know just yet, or her father. She might not accept my help."

Nikki blinked. "Wow. That's a great idea actually, but she said she might lose the land if they have to close the sanctuary."

"She only has to keep it running a couple more years. Do you think she is going to let anything close her down? Look at all she's done. She's willing to work with me to keep it open."

He took a deep breath and slowed his pounding heart. "Nothing is going to stop her, and if she lives there that's even better. With all her focus on the animals, what Danica always wanted has been lost with everything else she does for other people around here."

At least the couple wasn't staring at him with open hostility. They were easier to talk to than the rest of the Bergmann family. It was all the encouragement he needed. "On the first day, I saw the house, and she told me how she had planned to live there but didn't have the time or the resources to fix it."

Crossing the room, Adrian stopped in front of him. He was shorter than Reid, but he was solid and didn't look like a man you could push around. "Why are you doing this? What are you expecting in return?"

"I'm not playing a game. It is what it is. Danica wants to live in that house, and I want to give it to her. So, when she tells me it's time for me to move on, I can leave knowing they have a home of their own." He took a breath. This part was tougher. "I hope that her family, who happen to own a lumberyard, would help me make her dream come true."

Nikki joined her husband. Her stance was just as fierce. "No strings?" Her eyes narrowed.

"None."

Adrian crossed his arms. "What's your long-term plan?"

The Bergmanns were a family. A real family. The kind that supported each other no matter what. They were the only family his daughters would know, and he could sleep well knowing they were loved. Even if he couldn't be the one to love them.

He had done better than his father already. Now his only job was not to mess it up.

"I don't have long-term plans right now. I'm learning to live one day at a time. I start each morning with God, and try to keep Him in everything I do throughout the day."

Each word was painful. It went against Reid's instincts to talk about his personal business, but he needed someone in Danica's family to not see a total loser when they looked at him.

Adrian nodded. "We all make mistakes. How we get back on the right path is what matters. We don't know each other, but this is my family too now. Do you want to be a part of the girls' lives?"

He wanted to yell yes, but his father's words dragged across his brain like the jagged edge of a cut fence. There was no escaping who he was. His father's son. He clenched his fist. He wanted to be better, but could he be? Was it possible?

"Man, think about it carefully, because it's a serious commitment. Once they know you and love you, there is no going back without damaging them."

Nikki slugged him in the arm. "Adrian. Simmer. Mr. Never Missteps here tends to be a bit overprotective of the girls in his life. Between the two of us, I'm the one that made the huge mistakes. So I want to help you, but you need to understand that if you hurt my sister or my nieces, I will hunt you down, and I have the skills to do it."

"She does." Adrian slipped his arm around her waist. They made a solid wall. "So, what's the plan?"

"When it comes to telling the girls, I'll let Danica decide. Other than that, I want to do as much as I can while I'm here. I want to make the ranch house livable."

They nodded in unison. Adrian spoke. "So, how can we help with the Home for Danica Project?"

Reid smiled. "I've done construction and know my way around a basic job, but I thought you could look at the house and see if I'm missing any serious problems. I thought your dad might provide supplies. I'll pay, but I don't think he'd sell to me. Plus, I wasn't sure if he would fight the idea of her and the girls moving out."

"Let me see when I'm available." Adrian pulled out his phone and flipped through it. "Looks like the end of this week works."

Nikki smiled. "I'll take them to Kerrville for dinner. Let me take care of Daddy. I don't know why we haven't thought of this before now. She loves that place. It seems a bit obvious she should move into the house."

"Knowing her, she didn't want to bother anyone. It was a small fire, so hopefully, the structure is solid and not compromised."

"It's not going to take her long to figure out what's going on."

"I know, but I think once the plan is in motion, and the repairs are started, she'll be fine."

"This is a good thing you're doing." Nikki was the first Bergmann to look at him with something other than disdain. Of course, she hadn't been there the first time around.

Adrian held his hand out. At first, Reid didn't realize the man wanted to shake. He was an idiot, reaching forward to grasp Adrian's palm. His grip was firm.

The song "Wish Upon a Star" started playing from Adrian's pocket. Nikki laughed. "You need to get your daughter a new horse, or you're going to have to live with girly ringtones. She's ready for a faster horse." She turned to Reid. "That's his daughter's way of letting him know she is not happy about his decision."

"No. I'm not giving in to ringtone blackmail." Shaking his head, he walked out of the room as he answered his phone.

With nothing else to say, Reid dipped his head. "Thank you, Nikki. I'll talk to you later." He turned to leave.

"Wait." She lowered her voice. "Can I have a minute?"

Outside the oversize windows, clouds shrouded the sun, casting a darkness over the room. He knew better than to assume he could walk away without taking a hit. Planting a smile on his face, he turned back to her and waited. He would smile and stay calm, no matter what she thought he needed to know.

"You're not the first to walk out on her. There is a long line of people she loved and trusted that disappeared on her. Including me. So be patient. She's strong and independent, but more important, I'm afraid she's not going to let anyone close to the real her. You must know for sure if you're in this for keeps. Because you'll have to cross the Grand Canyon without a safety net to reach her."

"How do I make this right for both of us? My family history doesn't offer me a great deal of hope. I want..." His hands were cold. "I don't know if I can do what I want to do. I want to be a good family man and father, but what if it's not in my DNA? I have a screwed-up past. What I did to Danica is just part of it."

"God is in your DNA. With Him, your past does not have to be your future. I know that firsthand. I'm not a counselor like Adrian or any kind of spiritual leader, but I know God gave me a new beginning. I ran for about ten years. God brought me back here. To my family. To Adrian. To a community that I thought would reject me when they learned what I had done."

"I don't even know how to be part of a normal family."

She laughed. "There's no such thing as normal. On the surface, it looks all-American, but hang around, and you'll find out all our sordid secrets." She looked over her shoulder. "Except for Adrian."

"Don't listen to her." The male voice carried through the rooms. An edge of laughter floated right behind it. "I have issues, too. Just ask my daughter's mother."

"We're not talking to you," she yelled back so Adrian could hear, a smile on her face as she shook her head. "The point is all of us have messed up. Including my father, so don't let him fool you."

"If someone like me came around one of my daughters, I'd chase him off, too. Undoubtedly in a violent matter. Then I'd definitely be on the run."

"You're leaving? Where are you going?" Danica was on the stairs, concern and maybe even a little panic in her expression. "Reid, don't do anything to get yourself in more trouble. They'd throw you back in prison! I'm not taking my girls to visit you in jail."

Nikki chuckled. "That's what happens when you jump into a conversation midstream."

"I thought you wanted me to leave." Hope was a deadly thing.

She stood at the top of the stairs as if she might take off running.

He slowly moved toward her, but not so close that she'd bolt. "Are you thinking of letting me see the girls?" Words were hard to get past his dry throat.

"You've already met the girls. But that's not the point. Who were you going to chase in a violent manner?"

Nikki chuckled. "I'll let you handle this one, big guy. I'm sure Adrian needs my help with something."

Danica cut across the room to an old pine table. She wouldn't look at him as she ran her fingertips across the worn surface. "This belonged to my great-grandparents." She looked around the room. "This was the family living quarters in the early days."

"You didn't answer my question. Are you thinking of introducing me to our daughters?"

She crossed her arms. "And you didn't tell me who you wanted to fight. You know you're going to have to let insults slide, right? I noticed you're better at holding your temper than you were when I brought you home last time. So don't let anyone control your emotions. It's not worth it."

"Yes, ma'am." Hip on the table's edge, he crossed his arms and smiled at her. Just being in the same room with her was a gift. "We were talking about fathers and daughters. I told her if some punk like me showed any interest in one of my girls, I'd hit him. I didn't see it the first time we came to visit, but I have a much deeper appreciation for your father. He was right. You shouldn't have trusted me."

"If you stick around, the girls will have no chance of dating. Between you, my father and Adrian, no boy would be brave enough."

The need to be near her beat down his resistance. Not able to take the distance any longer, he worked his way around the table, until he stood next to her. Her fresh, sweet scent invaded him, reassured him.

He placed his hand where hers had just traced the wood pattern. It was still warm from her touch. Head down, he watched her hands. "Danica, I want to stay for the long haul. I do. I already missed six years. Years I'll never get back. Please, let me be here for the next fifteen." He swallowed and hoped she didn't hear the catch in his throat.

For what felt like an eternity, they stood in silence. Reid feared to take a breath.

Soft bells chimed from her pocket. Taking out her phone, she swiped the screen. "I need to go pick up the girls from school. One day a week, they get to go out and help feed the animals." Flipping her braid over her shoulder, she looked out the window. "Do you want to go with me? I could use the help. As a friend."

His heart slammed hard against his chest. "Yes. Thank you. I came into town with Wade, but I'll let him know I don't need a ride back to the ranch."

"Okay."

She already looked like she was regretting the invitation. Reid followed her down the steps. "I appreciate this. I know it's big for you to trust me this way." He struggled with ways to assure her. "I promise I won't say or do anything without your approval."

"I'm counting on that." Back on the store level, she retrieved her bag from under the counter. "Daddy, we're getting the girls and heading to the sanctuary."

Her father blocked the narrow hall that led to the back door. "We? He's not going with you."

Reid tried to stay calm, but as always, Mr. Bergmann brushed against his brittle ego. He closed his eyelids and breathed before opening them and meeting the man's gaze. Facing the grandfather of his daughters, Reid prayed for wisdom. He needed to earn this man's favor. So far, he hadn't done a thing to deserve that honor. His short fuse was his problem, not her father's.

Making sure to keep a glare from forming on his face, he waited for Danica. No big deal. He could do this. He forced his fists to relax, right along with his jaw.

Chapter Nine

Danica blew out some hot air, puffing her cheeks. Her father wasn't even looking at her. He was too busy staring down Reid at the back of the store. "Yes, Daddy. Reid is going with me to the sanctuary."

He crossed his long arms. His jaw twitched. "It's Tuesday."

God, please save me from the overprotective people in my life. "Yes, it is. Tomorrow is Wednesday."

"You don't need to get smart with me, girl."

Keys in hand, she walked toward Reid. "You didn't raise me to be stupid, Daddy."

Her father reached for her arm, stopping her. "The girls go with you on Tuesday. You're taking him to pick up the girls? Are you sure that's wise?"

She sighed and resisted the eye roll. Really, she was too old. "Daddy, please don't start." She looked around the store to make sure it was clear of any other ears. "He is their father, whether you like it or not."

"I don't like it. Don't go getting weak on me. It's not just you that he'll hurt this time." He grunted. "I feel like I'm repeating myself too much."

She glanced at Reid. He stood relaxed and calm. Not like he had just been insulted by her father. Wanting to encourage him, she smiled. If she still knew him, this was hard on his pride.

She hugged her father, then stepped around him. "Come on, Reid. Let's go."

"If you don't want to listen to me, maybe you want to live somewhere else."

This time she couldn't stop her eyes going

skyward. Reid looked worried. "He doesn't mean it."

"Danica! Don't go rolling your eyes at me. You're too old for that!"

She went back to her father. "I love you, but please don't treat me like I'm five." With a quick kiss on his cheek, she turned to leave. "Bye, Daddy. I'll see you for dinner tonight."

"You're not bringing him into my house."

With a sigh, she took Reid by the arm. "Do not engage. Just walk. I need to get my own place." She mumbled it under her breath, but she must have spoken louder than she thought.

"In good time, baby." Reid winked, his expression relaxed despite her father's surliness.

Her lungs threatened to stop working. This was the playful Reid she had fallen in love with. He held her car door open. The now-familiar seriousness quickly replaced his mischievous smile. "You sure about this? I don't want to cause more problems."

"Daddy will be okay." She paused before getting into the car. Straightening, she looked into his eyes. They were grayer today. "But no, I'm not sure. The last time I was sure about something, I ended up alone and pregnant." He had to know this was not easy for her.

"Danica…"

"Let's go before I change my mind."

It didn't take long to get the girls. Excited to see Reid, they chattered from the back seat the whole ride.

She slowed the car down.

"Momma! Why are you taking us home?"

"There's something I need to get at the house before we head out to the refuge."

Reassured, they went back to asking Reid a million questions and telling him all about their day at school.

They were so engaged in their rapid-fire conversation, no one asked her what was in the bag she put in the back. She wasn't even sure if she was going to give it to Reid. Maybe her father was right, and she was weak. Her resolution to keep Reid at a safe distance was already eroding.

Reid laughed as the girls told him who got in trouble at school, and who had the best lunches. As they pulled into the gates of the sanctuary, the girls started talking about the cub and the baby bats.

"Can we feed them, Momma?"

"Please. Can we help give them their baths?" As usual, the girls spoke at once.

"Girls, if you're very quiet, you can watch, but we don't want them getting used to a bunch of people." Danica parked and cut the engine before hopping out of the car with the rest of her crew. "They're wild animals, and we need them to go back into the wild."

The twins ran around to join her as she walked up to the building. "I want to live with the wild animals," Suzie said, and Lizzy nodded in agreement. They turned to Reid. "When we grow up, we are going to live with a wild animal and do research and make a TV show."

"We're going to be famous. The Wild Bergmann Sisters." They giggled. "We've designed the set and everything."

"You'll have to show me." Reid looked at her with that mischievous grin. "I have a surprise."

That expression used to make her giddy. Now it caused her stomach to drop, and not in a pleasant way. "Reid, what have you done?"

"Come on, and I'll show you." Reid moved past and held the door open for them. "I did it a couple of days ago, and you didn't even notice."

"What is it! What is it!" The girls jumped and danced inside in search of this big surprise Reid had supposedly prepared.

He walked farther into the room and picked up the old laptop to flip it open. With a few strokes of the keyboard, he turned the screen around for the girls to see. In unison, they leaned forward and then gasped as one.

"What is it?" Danica peered over the girls' shoulders.

"Look, they're wiggling." Suzie pointed to the bats on the screen.

"Oh." Her orphaned bats were on the laptop, streaming from a live feed. "Looks like it's feeding time. They're getting hungry." She went to the other room, scanning the area. High on the shelf was a small camera.

"Now you can watch them whenever you want without bothering them. Your mom can even log on with her phone, or on your computer at home. You can even go back a couple of days and watch what you missed."

"This is the most awesome thing ever!" Lizzy rushed at Reid and wrapped her arms around him. Suzie followed.

"Thank you, Mr. Reid. Thank you." And just as quickly, they went back to intently staring at the screen.

Danica shook her head. "You always loved

surprises. But now I'm afraid the girls aren't going to get anything done at the house." Prepared to turn and scowl at him, she had to pause at the look of wonder on his face. He was more into this than the girls, and they bounced with excitement.

His eyes glistened. He wiped at them with the back of his hand.

His jaw flexed, and then he gave her a thoughtful smile. "I'm sorry. I was going to show it to you first, but today took an unexpected turn for me. I thought it would be fun to surprise you all. Do you want me to take it down?"

"No!" Suzie's eyes teared up, making the gray shimmer. They looked so much like Reid's. She was losing her children to him. Was he doing this on purpose?

"No." Liz, the calmer one, took Danica's hand and squeezed it. "Please, Momma, we'll listen to you. We'll do our chores."

"It can stay, but we're going to make some rules for when and how long. Okay?"

"Yes, yes! This is the greatest!" Suzie jumped and returned to the screen. "Look, the little one is licking the one next to him." Their laughter was magical. Even on her worst day, it was the one thing that could soothe her.

Liz gave Reid another hug. "We love it. Thank you!"

Head to head, they stared at the screen. "Girls, you stay here while I feed and bathe them, okay?"

"Okay, Momma." They answered in unison as usual.

Reid stood. "I'll go feed the cub."

They all went about their chores. After a while, she gathered the girls and went to the front porch. Using the walkie-talkie, she called Reid for his location.

"Back at the bear enclosure. Are you ready to go?" His voice was low.

"Girls, do you want to see the cub before we leave?" She smiled as they danced and clapped. It was a ridiculous question. She spoke into the walkie-talkie. "We'll come join you, then leave from there."

"Do we get to ride the Mule?" Another of their favorite activities, riding the all-terrain vehicle.

"Sure. Climb on." With the girls buckled into the back seat, they took off. Over the last hill, the enclosure became visible. Slowing down, she parked the vehicle off at a distance, so as not to bother the cub too much. "Remember, girls, stay quiet."

"Yes, ma'am." They all climbed off, as quietly as possible.

When they reached to the fence, the girls wrapped their fingers between the chain links. "Oh, Mr. Reid, the baby bear thinks you're her daddy."

The bear had gotten bigger but still loved cuddling against Reid's chest. She was holding her bottle as he rocked her.

Suzie looked at her mom. "Do bears stay with their dads?"

"No, bears are raised by their mothers."

"Just like us, but this bear has Reid."

All of a sudden, their innocent words clawed into her heart. She made the mistake of glancing at Reid. Would she ever stop losing her breath when he looked back at her? Her heart started racing. The girls never talked about their lack of a father. It was just the way of life for them.

"I'm not her father. Just a caregiver, until she can be on her own."

"Isn't that what a father does?" her older daughter asked.

"How much longer will she need you to take care of her?" Her sister didn't want to be left out of the conversation.

"Your mom is the one who mainly takes care of her, and gave her a safe place to grow up. She just likes it when I get to feed her." Bottle empty, he sat her on the thick branch that stretched across the pen. He ducked under it and came to the gate, exiting the enclosure. The cub rolled down to the ground, then clambered to the top of the little cave like structure. From there, she crossed to the smaller branch. Running, as if being chased, she leaped into the small water tank.

The girls laughed at the cub's antics. "She's so funny."

They asked another hundred questions while they watched the baby bear scurry around. The bear even ambled to the fence and stuck her nose through. The girls giggled with delight.

The light softened as the sun started slipping behind the western hills. "Girls, we need to go. We have to take Reid to his ranch before we go home."

"Can he come have dinner with us?"

"No, not tonight."

"Maybe another night?" The twins pouted, pleading with their eyes.

She looked at Reid over the heads of their daughters. The loneliness and yearning in his eyes hurt her heart. "Maybe."

"Yay!" They raced to the four-wheeler Reid had come on.

"Can I ride with Mr. Reid?" Suzie asked.

"No! I want to!" Lizzy frowned at her sister.

"Neither of you are going with him. There aren't any seat belts on his four-wheeler."

"Oh, Mom. He'll drive slow, right?" Lizzy looked at him.

Danica raised one eyebrow and put her hands on her hips. "I don't think he does anything slow."

He swung the girls up and planted them on the big Mule's back seat. "I think your mom means business."

The girls grumbled. "She always means business."

"Because she loves you. Do you know how blessed you are to have such a great mom? Not everyone gets a mom likes yours."

Liz nodded. "Our friend Celeste, her mother's dead. Travis, a boy in our class, his mom yells at everyone."

Suzie leaned forward. "She's crazy. Once the police had to come get her at school."

"Girls, stop. That's gossip. It's not nice to talk about people. If you're worried about your friend, we need to tell someone."

"It's not gossip. We saw it. Everyone knows." Suzie looked at her mother. "That's not gossip."

With a frown, Lizzy nodded. "It happened at school. Poor Travis. His dad, Mr. Monardo, was arrested. He's in jail." She looked at her sister. "Maybe that part is gossip."

They started talking about what gossip meant. "Girls, that's enough. When it is other people's business, it's gossip. Unless there are ways we can help them, we shouldn't be talking about them." She'd heard the same gossip in town, but she didn't know Travis's family. Talking about them behind their back made her uncomfortable.

She made a note to ask Pastor Levi.

"Travis Monardo?" The girls nodded at Reid's question. "There's a man in my group by that name."

"Group?"

Oh, no. She needed to derail this conversation. "We should head home before it gets too dark. Come on, let's go."

Instead of going to his four-wheeler, Reid went down to sit on his heels and look the girls in the eye. "I'm in a group that studies the Bible with Pastor Levi. We have all been in prison."

Both girls' eyes went wide. "You? You were in jail?"

"What for?"

"Suzie, that's not a polite question." Danica put on her seat belt. This was becoming dangerous territory.

"It's okay." He smiled at the girls. "I had a problem, and instead of waiting for God's time, I tried to take a shortcut to make money. I broke the law. I served my time, and I'm working hard to make better choices."

Liz touched his face. "Opa says if you turn your problems over to God, He'll forgive and get you back on the right path."

"Your opa is a very smart man."

Suzie reached for his hand. "He also says it's easier to stay on the right path and not get lost than having to find your way back."

"Easier to stay out of trouble than to get out of trouble." Lizzy lowered her voice and gained a bit of a German accent, sounding just like her grandfather.

He laughed. "Now, those are some words of wisdom I hope you try to follow. It's true. So stay out of trouble."

"Are you still in trouble?" Lizzy tilted her head.

"I'm working to prove I can be trusted. It's a long road, but I'm on it."

"We trust you." Both girls nodded.

His arms went around the girls. "Thank you. That means a lot to me."

Danica couldn't take it anymore. Gripping the steering wheel with one hand, she cleared her throat and blinked the tears away. With her other hand, she started the engine. She needed to put distance between them.

Suzie and Lizzy gave their trust without

ever having had it betrayed. Her job was to make sure they got through their childhood without any scars on their sweet hearts.

"Look, if we stay any longer, the sun will be in bed before we get home. Opa will worry about us."

He nodded and turned away, heading back to his four-wheeler.

As fast as she could, Danica drove the girls back to the main sanctuary house and loaded them into the Suburban. Reid pulled up behind them and shut off the four-wheeler before climbing into the passenger seat of the SUV. He seemed to have read her mood and let the girls talk about a project they were doing at school.

It didn't take too long before they were pulling through the ornate entrance of the Hausman ranch. Past the main house and elaborate stables, she stopped in front of a row of old cabins. Cowboys hung out on the porches.

"Which one do you live in?"

"The last one." He pointed.

"It's like a little town for cowboys." Suzie sounded way too excited about the idea of cowboys.

"That reminds me, I won't be out at the reserve at all on Saturday. We have some big corporate event, and they need all hands on deck. We have to make sure that none of the city folks injure themselves as we drive the cattle from the west pasture to the back five hundred."

"Sounds fun?" Sounded like something he would hate.

"Yeah, horses and animals I can handle all day. People? Not my thing. I'd rather be hanging out with bats and bears, but we'll get it done. Thanks for the ride. Bye, girls."

"Bye, Mr. Reid. Thank you for the bat cam."

"You're welcome." Out of the car, he turned and leaned in, grinning at the girls. "Don't make your mother get mad at me because you aren't doing your chores."

"We promise."

If she was going to show him the photos, she had to do it now. Would it send the wrong message? The door started closing. "Oh, Reid. Wait! I have something for you. It's in the back."

Hopping out of the Suburban, she ran to the back. Some of the cowboys hollered out a greeting. She waved in a hurry. A few joked about Reid's date bringing him home, the others mentioned the cute chaperones in the back seat.

He shook his head, shutting the passenger's door. "Sorry about that."

"Don't worry about it. Remember, I grew up here at the lumberyard. I know how cowboys can be." She opened the back door and pulled out the large bag by its handles.

A line was being crossed that she couldn't undo as she passed on her memories of the last six years.

"What's this?" Taking it in both hands, he opened it and looked down. Just as quick, his gaze shot back up. "Is this what I think it is?"

Biting at her lips, she nodded. "It's the scrapbooks I started with my first doctor appointment. The first sonogram when we saw two heartbeats." She had to stop talking, because she couldn't cry here. Not with all the cowboys watching.

"Hey, Reid. She giving you enough food to share?"

What had she been thinking? This was not the place to give these to him.

She kept her gaze down, focused on his hands. There was no way she could look at his face. "There's one book for each year. It goes up to their first day of kinder." Pulling away, she crossed her arms and looked off toward the lights of the main house.

The only thing saving her dignity was the dark. The lights from the porches didn't reach them.

Danica sighed, relaxing. "There's a flash drive with movies of them rolling, crawling, walking. It's gone by so fast. You can keep the flash drive, but I need the scrapbooks back."

"Of course." His voice was rough and low.

She wasn't daring enough to hug him, let alone look at him. If she touched him now, she might never let go. He reached up to touch her face, and she stepped back. "Well, I have to go. The girls are waiting."

"All right." Good-natured ribbing and jokes were thrown his way as Reid followed her to the driver's side and shut the door. She didn't look his way, making sure to keep her gaze straight ahead.

Why did it feel like she just gave him her heart again? She didn't. They were just pictures of her daughters. His daughters. That was all. He was their father.

It didn't mean she was going to fall in love with him again. She couldn't. Once someone left her that was it. They never came back.

* * *

He was sure the guys called out to him, making stupid jokes, but the blood pounding in his ears was all he heard. In his hands, he held the lives of his daughters.

Danica had given him all their milestones and everyday wonders. Hoping he looked casual, Reid made his way to his room after watching the Suburban drive off. The front steps seemed so far away. The porch was longer than it was this morning. The door wouldn't open. His roommates had locked the door? No one ever locked anything around here. It usually drove him crazy, but of course, they'd locked it this one time when all he wanted was to go inside and be alone with his new gift. He resisted the urge to beat his fist against at the door.

While fumbling for the keys, his breathing became hard. He needed to get into his room and devour each picture, each snippet of life he'd missed while locked away.

The door finally opened. Now to get to his room.

The fourteen-by-fifteen space was bigger than his cell, yet he felt suffocated. With slow, steady movements, he sat the bag on the empty nightstand between his bed and an old ranch chair.

He went back and closed the door. Something he hadn't done since the day he first sat his duffel bag on the bed.

It wasn't rational, but every nerve in his body rebelled at the thought of being locked inside again. The idea that he could get up and walk out anytime still felt raw. Too unreal.

Yet this moment with his girls was his alone. He didn't want anyone interrupting. They'd respect a closed door.

Taking a deep breath, he sat down and peered into the bag. There were five binders, each one with a date written in fancy lettering. He pulled out the oldest one. Susan

Marie Bergmann and Elizabeth Ann Bergmann were inscribed on the cover.

His fingertips hovered over the names of his daughters. Would they ever know his name? Would they be ashamed to be a McAllister?

The spine creaked as he opened the book. Page by page, he watched Danica's belly grow to the point it looked impossible. Her sisters Jackie and Samantha were in many of the pictures. From baby showers to the trip to the hospital.

Then the girls, both in pink. One wore stripes, and the other was dressed in polka dots. So tiny. Time ceased to exist as he stared at them. How could the girls he knew have started out so small?

He tried to imagine holding them. They would have fit in the palm of his hand. His lungs burned. Everything he missed, and there was no one to blame but himself. One stupid shortcut and he'd lost all of this.

He quickly wiped away moisture that

gathered in the corner of his eyes. By the end of the first book, the girls were standing. Laying that one on the bed, he picked up the next one.

With snaggletoothed grins, they were proudly walking. Their hair was finally growing. They wore their red curls in funny little pigtails on the top of their heads.

At this point, they had started feeding themselves, and not effectively. There looked to be more tomato sauce and noodles on them than on their plates. More than ever now, he wanted to make that house ready for them. Even if he never got to live in it with them, his love would be embedded within the walls.

The last book was incomplete. Blank pages waiting to be filled with new memories. He wanted to be on those pages. Laying his palm flat against the empty pages, he prayed. He slipped from the chair and fell to his knees, head bowed.

He prayed for his girls. All three of them. He prayed for their protection. And he prayed for peace.

Chapter Ten

The sun was just waking up. Reid had his favorite cold drink, and the day ahead looked good. For two weeks, he and Bobby had secretly been working inside the house. Today was going to be big. They wouldn't be able to hide the secret project any longer. Philip and Wade, the two cowboys he lived with, rode shotgun on the way to do some major work on the house. It humbled him the way the other cowboys stepped in and helped whenever he needed. No questions asked. They were also doing it for her.

Philip had gone to school with Danica.

Wade knew her from the church. So, of course, they were more than happy to help. "Thank you, guys, for volunteering. With extra hands, we can make a huge dent in restoring the house."

"Glad to help. Didn't have anything else to do today." Philip took a slow sip of his coffee from the biggest insulated metal cup he'd ever seen.

Wade yawned. "Tearing down walls sounds more fun than burning cactus."

"There's a bunch, so it's cacti," Philip informed him.

"No. It's not a Latin word. It's German." Wade went on to explain the difference.

Reid chuckled. They would argue over anything and loved every minute. Despite that, he hoped they would get everything done today. Jackie had taken Danica and the girls into San Antonio. Adrian had gathered up some volunteers from the church, but there was still so much to get finished.

He took another long drink of Big Red. He needed to calm down. It was all going to work out. By the end of the day, when she saw the house, it would be too late for her to tell them to stop.

That was the plan anyway. Would Danica get mad at him, or smile at him like she used to back when his life was good? When they were dating, he'd lived to surprise her, and she'd loved it. Her laughter and her smile had made him believe anything was possible, that he could outrun his father's legacy.

"Yo, McAllister," Philip hollered at him.

He glanced in the rearview mirror. "Sorry. I didn't hear you." Lost in thought, he'd missed the conclusion of the debate.

"Who else is going to be there?" Wade asked.

"Not sure. Nikki, Adrian and George will be there for sure. He said some others would be coming, too."

Pulling up to the ranch road, he stopped for a truck to pass. On the door was the Bergmann Lumber logo. It was pulling a flatbed loaded with lumber and panels. In the back of the truck, there were large boxes that looked like appliances. Nikki must have gotten her father to help on the project because Reid certainly didn't have enough money for all those supplies. His heart pounded.

Following the truck through the gate, he hit the brake hard out of shock. There weren't just a few cars, but a full parking lot. A horn honked behind him. He was blocking the road. Refocusing, he drove forward and found an empty spot in the back next to the old pecan tree.

Wade whistled. "Looks like I wasn't the only one avoiding pasture work."

Philip laughed as he got out of the front seat. He stood at the hood of the truck. "I remember this place. I used to make money mowing the old lady Edward's lawn. She always paid me extra."

Mr. Bergmann stepped out of the truck with Nikki and Samantha. Joaquin was with them, too. He started untying the lumber in the flatbed. "Where do we unload?"

Nikki started directing people. With her in charge, no one had a chance to stand still and be useless. She put everyone to work. Reid found Adrian and got the update on all the people. Apparently, more were arriving.

In work overalls and a beat-up baseball cap, Samantha stomped over to them. "I need something to do that's dangerous."

Reid looked to Adrian to handle this problem. He didn't even know where to begin.

Adrian grinned. "What did he say you can't do?"

"Apparently, I'm too weak to unload the manly lumber. I grew up in a lumberyard!" She threw her hands in the air. "Do I look too fragile to handle hard work?" She put her hands on her hips. "And don't try to humor me. I'm a grown woman who knows what I'm capable of doing."

"What about the roof? Not only is it hard work, but he'll see you up there working, and you won't have to say a word."

"Yes." She hugged his neck. "You're the best brother-in-law." She turned. "Oh, Reid. Well, you're not my brother-in-law, you're the girls' father but… I mean I like you, too, I just…"

"Get out of here before you embarrass yourself even more." Adrian pointed to the west toward his twin brother. "George is in charge of all things roofing."

"Sorry. Everyone knows I have no social skills." She stomped away, her long braid swinging. Turning, she walked backward. "Make sure to tell my sister I fixed that lame gate motor for her."

Reid nodded at her, then looked at Adrian. "Mr. Bergmann limits the kind of work she does?" That surprised him. "All the girls seem to know their way around the lumberyard."

"No. It's not her dad." The laugh lines around his eyes went deeper. "Joaquin teases her, and she takes the bait every time. Between you and me, they would be much happier if they'd just admit they liked each other. It's like they're still in fourth grade."

Not knowing how to respond to that, Reid shrugged. "Adrian, this is so much more than I expected. Where did all these people come from?"

"Most of them from the church. The sanctuary also has quite a few friends. Plus, Danica's family has been a cornerstone of this community. Getting the opportunity to give back to them is rare, and people want to help."

The sheriff's patrol car pulled into the drive. Reid scanned the area. Had he done something wrong? He planted his feet, crushing the urge to run.

"You've met Jake Torres, right?" Adrian waved to the lawman. "He used to do construction and help renovate several houses in the county."

There was no way Reid would ever feel comfortable around anyone in a uniform. As a kid, he was taught they were out to get him. Then they did get him. Now after serving time? They made his skin feel too tight. With an easy smile on his face, Adrian greeted Sheriff Torres, then turned to Reid.

Every breath was focused with intention. Reid made sure to relax his tense muscles before shaking hands.

"I hear you need an electrician?"

Adrian answered first. "The damage doesn't look too extensive. The plan is to get the appliances installed before Danica shows up later today. Mr. Bergmann has all the needed supplies. Reid, will you show him the way? I'll check the lumber for rebuilding the back porch."

From there, the day went fast. Sounds of hammers, drills and laughter filled the air.

He helped replace windows and doors. People came and went all day long.

Every few hours someone showed up with food. It was the most amazing thing he'd ever seen. At times, it felt as if he was invisible, watching all the activity from the outside. Everyone knew everyone else's name. It was one big messy family.

New counters went into the kitchen as he stepped back to look at the work. Someone he didn't know offered him and everyone else in the room a drink. "They look great with the cabinets. Danica is going to love this."

Reid took a drink. There were too many people. Needing some fresh air, and silence, he walked to the big pecan tree at the back of the yard.

The need to pray was overwhelming. He didn't belong here, not with all these good, hardworking people. Why were they so friendly? By now, they must know he'd been in prison.

Yanking the aviators off his face, Reid braced his hands on the hood of the truck and bowed his head. He let the words flow as he gave the Lord thanks. He turned his fears and insecurities over to God. Ray had told him forgiveness was his when he asked, but he didn't know how that was possible. His mistakes felt like grooves in his hide that he'd never be able to sand down.

Boots crunched the grass behind him. Fists clenched, he turned. Danica's father frowned at him. His father-in-law. The grandfather of his children. He lowered his hand, flexing his fingers. "Sorry."

The man who probably hated him more than anyone else, and with good reason, stood before him.

"You okay?" The subtle edge of the old German accent was proof of his connection to this community. The Bergmanns had roots that ran deep. They couldn't be more different as people.

Mr. Bergmann stared at him, waiting for

a response. Reid's lack of words made for an awkward moment. "Yeah." He had a hard time meeting the man's narrowed gaze. "All the people coming and going is a bit unsettling. I just needed a moment alone."

"I'm not big on crowds, either." Crossing his arms, he looked back to the house for a moment. Another awkward silence lingered between them.

Reid figured it was better than saying something stupid. So he let it drag out.

Clearing his throat, the older man studied Reid for a bit. "All this—" he jabbed his thumb over his shoulder "—it's a good thing you're doing, but I want to make it clear, I'm not going to forgive you. Don't ever expect me to welcome you into my family. You did enough damage to last a lifetime."

Not his family. Acid burned in the pit of his gut. "I know." They were in good hands. "Thank you."

His thick eyebrows shot up. "Thank you?" Hard eyes narrowed again. "For what?"

"For protecting my girls when I walked out on them. For being there for them and loving them. I…" He had no idea how to articulate what he was feeling. "Ray told me there are times in our lives we don't even know what prayer we need. So, we trust God has us. We praise him for it all. Good and bad. Even our unspoken prayer will be answered." Reid took a deep breath. "I don't know if this makes sense, but Danica was always in my prayers. I made a mistake, but she paid the price for my sin. I don't want to imagine what would have happened to her and the girls if you hadn't taken care of her the way I should have done."

"She's my daughter." His jaw tightened. "The best a father can hope for is that his children find happiness. When they don't, I hope they can come to me." The older man looked down. "I'm not always easy, but I love them." The eyes that looked so much like Danica's stared hard at him again. "I'll protect them with everything I have. It seems at times I have to protect them from themselves. Danica has worked hard to take her life back and to become a great mother. I'm not allowing you to pull her or my granddaughters down into your muck again."

He knew it was all truth, but it was always hard to deal with rejection. "I promised her I would be leaving as soon as she found a vet tech to replace me. I'll stay on the Hausman ranch, and out of her life. It's the least I can do. And I understand where you're coming from. If some man treated Suzie or Lizzy the way I treated Danica, well, I'd probably be in jail again. So, thank you."

Someone laughed in the background. He turned to watch the commotion. People were still so busy working to make this shell of a house into a home.

Reid smiled. "Your granddaughters don't know how cruel the world can be, and that's because of you. At their age, I knew how to call 911 when my mother took too many pills and how to ice her lip from the hit she took from her latest boyfriend. I learned to hide the guns and grocery money when my older brothers stopped by the house. Children should never have to grow up that way, acting like the adult. Thankfully, the girls won't have to develop those survival skills. So yeah, thank you."

The look of contempt on Mr. Bergmann's face shifted. Reid rolled his shoulders. He didn't need anyone's pity. His life was just what it was—his life. Like thousands of other kids'. But not his girls, because they had Danica and this man scowling at him.

Reid gestured to the house. "Looks like they're unloading the appliances. That's my cue to get back to work." He nodded at Danica's father and left to join the others once again. No more moping.

In the house, all evidence of the fire was erased. It was coming along great. His throat tightened.

"The floors look great." Vickie, the sheriff's wife, stood on the counter, hanging some fancy curtains over the window. "I can't believe how much work was finished without her knowing."

Philip laughed. "Reid hasn't slept in two weeks. I'm surprised no one called to report suspicious activity."

"Oh, I thought it was Bobby and Adrian."

Reid shifted on his feet. He didn't want people to know how much he had put into this project. They might start asking questions.

Sheriff Torres walked up to him and patted his back. "They did. The first time I showed up, I thought he was going to run." He looked up at his wife and frowned. "You shouldn't be up there."

She rolled her eyes. "It's way too early for you to get this bossy. This is my third pregnancy. I think I know what I can handle."

Jake moved closer, glaring at her. "Well, it's my first, so you'll just have to deal with it. Let me help you down."

"As soon as I'm finished you can carry me

off caveman style, but not until then. Help the guys get the refrigerator hooked up."

Shaking his head, the sheriff grinned at him. "Pregnant women are hard to deal with."

Reid nodded like he knew anything about it. Had Danica climbed up on high places? Had anyone helped her down?

With help, they slid the big black appliance into its new home. Sheriff Torres went to his wife and with one gentle motion had her safely standing on the ground. A quick kiss was added to the movement, making Reid feel a little guilty for being in the room with them.

Philip's smirk didn't help. Then the room went silent. The hairs on the back of his neck itched. His back was to the door. Slowly, he turned and came eye to eye with Danica.

She scanned the area. Confusion, awe and shock tumbled across her face. Her attention shifted to him. Everything and everyone blurred on the edges of his brain. He could see her beautiful mind working, but he couldn't tell if it was good or bad.

"Surprise?" He straightened and took the gloves off.

"You did this?" She didn't move, just stood there staring at him, her fingers clenched around the leather strap of her bag. The large open kitchen got smaller as the number of people doubled.

Samantha rushed in from the front door and threw herself at Danica. "Isn't this amazing? Surprise!" She laughed and held her sister at arm's length.

Envy crept into his blood. He wanted to hug his wife and stand next to her with pride.

The youngest Bergmann entwined her arm through her sister's. "Let me show you what we've done. Everyone's been working since sunup. There is even a new roof."

With Samantha dragging her sister through the room, people started laughing and smiling. Shouts of thanks went back and forth. Everyone crowded the house to talk to her, to show her what part they had in the makeover.

The open door was calling to him. Easing his way outside, he tried to fade into the background. Air was hard to find.

"Mr. Reid!"

As one, the twins greeted him with arms wide-open. He went down on his haunches so he could return the hugs. For a moment, he held them tighter than necessary. He knew they greeted everyone in their world with such enthusiasm, but for this moment he imagined it was just for him. For this moment, he pretended they were a family, all of them together at their home.

Jackie walked up behind them. She was looking at the house. "Wow. There are people everywhere, and the house actually looks livable."

He stood. "It's almost there. Another week and it'll be ready."

"Ready for what?" The girls looked up. Their gazes darted between him and their aunt.

Reid placed his hands on top of their little heads. "We're fixin' the house for you and your mom to live in."

"Really?"

"We'll live with the animals?" They both clapped. Both of them took one of his hands and pulled him to the house. "Is Momma already inside?"

Lizzy suddenly stilled. The whole group stopped with her as she stared at her sister. "Wait. We'll still be in the same room, right? Do we have to sleep alone now?"

Jackie rubbed her red curls. "You get to share a room as long as you'd like."

The girls let go of him and ran ahead.

"Did you and Danica share a room?" he asked Jackie. Her glare sliced him, making it clear she didn't want to talk to him about her sister.

After a moment, she shook her head. "We

did until my father remarried. Shelia believed we needed to learn to be apart and made us move into separate rooms, but she found out we were slipping into Nikki's room and all sleeping together. She told us we weren't dogs. The next night, she started locking our doors."

Her jaw flexed, making her look just like her father. "Wanting to be as close as possible, we slept on the floor against the door that separated our new rooms. We could always see a bit of each other through the gap under the door. It was enough."

Gleams of tears hugged her lashes. With an even harder glare, she turned on him. "I'm not going to let anyone hurt her ever again." Without giving him an opportunity to say a word, she stomped off after the girls.

There were two Bergmanns that would never accept him. How would it feel to have family that loved him as much as they loved Danica?

The thought of a tiny Danica locked away

from her sisters, alone and curled up on the floor, tore at his heart. He pictured her against the door, wanting out and not being able to get to the sisters she loved so much. Her support system. He was glad this Sheila woman was gone from their lives.

Hands in his pocket, he made his way to the house. It was probably time to go back inside, but all the people put him on edge.

"Reid?"

He lifted his head and stopped walking. Danica stood on the top step. Arms crossed, she frowned at him. What had he done now?

"Are you going to be antisocial for the rest of the day?" Hopping down the few short steps, she strode toward him as if she had a mission. "You did this?"

Pointing to all the vehicles, he avoided her eyes. "There are beaucoup people here putting this all together."

"Stop it." She wrapped her fingers around his hand and lowered it. "Adrian told me you went to him and asked for help to get this…" Her lips tightened, and she blinked a few times. Taking a deep breath, she released his hand and crossed her arms over her chest.

The warmth was gone. Danica took a step back and looked at the house. "You asked for help to get this done before you had to leave. You even asked my father for help."

"Everyone loves you. You never let anyone help. I thought Adrian should take the lead. Then no one would wonder why the ex-con was building a home for the hometown sweetheart." Anger bubbled up. He loved her but had to act like she didn't matter to him. "I asked what it would take. Next thing I know, it seems like the whole town decided to do some sort of old-fashioned barn raising."

"Thank you." Pulling her sweater closer around her, she chewed on her top lip. He shrugged. The silence grew heavy. She scanned the yard. "The girls have already picked out a room."

"Do they want pink and green like their other room?" He needed to start moving, so he headed to the porch. "I'm going to start painting the bedrooms and living room. Thought you'd want to pick out the colors since you own a lumberyard."

She grinned and followed him. "Jackie is the color expert."

On the porch, he paused. "Yeah, your sister already gave me the list of colors, but I thought you might want to choose the colors you wanted. I know you're twins, but you seem so different to me."

"Really?" She stopped and turned to face him, leaning against the closed door. "Most people still can't tell us apart. I'll have whole conversations with people before I realize they think I'm Jackie."

"That's crazy."

"Reid, thank you." She reached out and put her hand on his forearm. The heat seeped right through his cotton shirt. "This is the most thoughtful thing anyone has ever done for me."

Hope was deadly. The higher it lifted his heart, the harder the fall would be when this was over. But if these moments were all he got, then it was worth it. His blood pounded in his ears as he leaned forward. His hands went to her arms.

The door behind her opened. Reid's hold tightened to stop her from falling backward. Her father loomed behind her, glowering at him. Knowing she was sound on her feet, he let go and stepped back.

What had he been thinking? He was an idiot.

Mr. Bergmann stepped to the side, and Danica slipped past him. He shifted slightly, blocking Reid's entry. "I thought I made myself clear earlier."

"Yes, sir. We were talking paint colors when you opened the door." Every instinct told him to look down, avoid confrontation. But the need to be seen as a man overrode his survival instincts. For an eternity, they stood in the silent standoff. "I understand I'm unworthy of her. My father made that clear."

Mr. Bergmann's eyes narrowed.

"If you want me to leave now, I'll have to collect Philip and Wade." He wanted to stay and watch her move through the house he was making for her, but if it was going to cause a scene, he'd leave.

"That's a good idea. It's getting late. And the fewer people that see you around the girls, the better."

The anger that lived in his gut flared again. He wasn't sure if it was aimed at the man who was keeping him from his family or at himself. Taking a deep breath, he turned it over to God.

It was the only thing that ever worked. It still burned, but the rage was low and controllable now.

Finally, the older man moved to the side. He nodded and went inside. Walking through the kitchen, he smiled at the people. Philip and Wade were working in the master bath.

"Hey, guys, you ready to leave?"

James looked at his watch. "We still got a couple of hours of daylight."

"Mr. Reid, have you seen our room?" Suzie's mop of red curly hair popped out from the doorway across from the master room.

"Is this the one you picked?" He stepped inside. It was the room with the large window seat. He had already pictured the girls in this room. There would be enough space for two beds, dressers, dolls and dancing. Or whatever it was little girls spent their time doing.

Sheriff Torres held Lizzy. Danica and Vickie sat in the window seat looking at something in Vickie's lap.

"They're picking out material." Suzie ran back and crawled next to her mother.

Lizzy looked at the man holding her. "Thank you for your help. I better get over there, or Suzie will pick out crazy things."

Laughing, the sheriff bent down and let her go. He looked back at Reid, studying his face. "You have some unusual eye color there. Is it gray? Green?"

Reid touched his cheek, only just realizing he'd left his sunglasses outside on the hood of the truck. He'd gotten so distracted by prayer and Mr. Bergmann that he'd forgotten to put the aviators back on. And leave it to the lawman to be the first to notice. Panic settled in deep, tightening his chest. "Just an eye color. Nothing special."

"Right." The sheriff was shorter than Reid, but he didn't lack power. Feet planted, he crossed his arms and stared at him. The authority of a man who knew he was on the right side of God. "I guess if Danica wanted us to know, she'd say something."

Cold sweat broke out over Reid's entire body. Ignoring the comment, he made his way to the window. "Danica, I'm leaving. Got to get back to the ranch."

She stood. "I just got here." Disappointment pulled at her mouth. That's what he saw anyway. The expectation that he could have more would destroy him faster than anything that had happened to him in prison.

He wanted to tell her how much he missed her, how much he loved her. How she filled his thoughts and dreams every single day and night.

"I'm scheduled to be here tomorrow." That was safe and not so lame. His feet refused to turn. Like an idiot, he just stood there and waited for something that wasn't going to happen.

"I'm going now… Bye."

She tilted her head as if he was a puzzle with pieces missing. "Bye."

With a nod, Reid left. He walked out before he did something stupid. Maybe he needed to call Ray and get the prayer warrior on his side. It was a dangerous slope he was slipping down. Wanting more than what he deserved had gotten him in trouble too many times in the past. Homes and nice families were not for men like him.

Chapter Eleven

A week had passed since the surprise, and Danica was still floored. She paused before stepping into the room that would soon be for Suzie and Lizzy. Steadying her breath, she leaned against the doorframe and watched Reid carefully place the white trim along the edge of the ceiling. He reached up from the top of the ladder. One of her favorite songs came over the radio, and he started singing and swaying to the beat.

She smiled. They had spent so much time dancing in his small apartment. Being poor students, they hadn't had the money to go anywhere, but that had never stopped them from having fun.

Straightening, she shook her head. Memories were dangerous. All the pain was filtered out. Why was she so weak when it came to Reid?

He had painted varying stripes of pink against the soft white walls. A pretty green wainscoting surrounded the room. The time and detail he put in showed a man who cared.

This was all done without any promises from her. She hesitated to get his attention. After all these weeks, she'd gotten used to him being around. Now it was over, and she didn't like the heaviness that sat on her shoulders. What would happen if he wanted to stay? If they told the girls who he was?

She closed her eyes. The board meeting hadn't gone well last night. Her phone vibrated, and the slight noise brought Reid's head around.

"Danica." He smiled.

She looked down at her phone. Jackie had texted her.

Are you in the house with Reid?

After a pause, another text came through, and her notification went off again.

Please tell me you're not alone with him.

She didn't want to deal with her sister, the board or Reid. Running away and hiding sounded good, but she had to be an adult.

Her phone went off again.

You're not responding. You're with him, aren't you?

Jackie hadn't even given her time to respond.

Don't do anything stupid. I'm on my way.

"Your phone is doing a great deal of talking." He turned so that he sat astride the top of the four-foot ladder. One gorgeous eye-brow went up. "Are you going to answer?"

"It's Jackie." Treating her like a child. She slipped the phone into her back pocket, but the notification buzzing kept up a steady pace.

"You're not talking to your sister?"

"She's a few minutes older and seems to think that means she can lecture me like a child."

"It's about me, then. What did I do now?"

"Apparently, you exist."

"I don't think there's a way for me to fix that problem. Sorry." His lopsided grin slipped into place.

The phone went off again. She could not stop the eye roll this time.

He chuckled and leaned forward over the top of the ladder. "Maybe you should an-swer? Just a suggestion."

"If I ignore it, she'll give up."

"Or rush here to save you from the ex-con. How did the board meeting go last night? Anything new with the sheriff's investigation?"

"Nothing new in the investigation. They're interviewing some of the local ranchers who filed a complaint about the animals." She tried to think of a way to talk about the other complaints without hurting him. Sighing, she walked into the room. "Some board members have concerns with a convicted criminal working unsupervised. There's some talk that the problems began when you started working here."

His face went into the stone mode. Not even a single flex in the hard jaw. Those moss gray eyes turned cold. "What do you think about that?"

"It's ridiculous. I was tempted to tell them we were married, but that would only make matters worse. I just want to get that grant. Then I'll have the financial backing to fix everything else."

"You'll get it. But I think the sheriff might suspect the girls are mine."

A headache ruptured in her head. This was getting too complicated. She had stalled enough. "There's a reason I'm here. We found a volunteer for the vet tech job." There, she'd said it. The words burned her throat, but she kept her smile in place. Arms crossed, she looked everywhere but at him. They had agreed to this plan, to replace him as soon as possible. To get him out of her life.

"So, this is it. You don't need me anymore." Swinging his leg over the ladder, he jumped down. The sun from the tall window haloed him. "There's still some things I need to do to finish the house. And outside. I haven't even started in the yard yet. I want to fix the fence, and redo that fancy little gate."

"I grew up in the lumberyard. I think I can handle it. Plus, I have my dad, Adrian, my sisters, Bobby, Joaquin, James—"

"I get it."

Pulling her bottom lip in between her teeth, Danica thought about how calm her life was before Reid showed up in her office without warning. Now she lived in a constant state of turmoil.

He tossed the hammer into his toolbox. From across the room, the heat of his now-gray eyes froze her in place.

Breaking the hold, she focused on the renewed wood floor, all evidence of fire and water damage erased. The old carpet and musty smell were gone. Adrian told her the carpet had protected the old floors.

The smell of a freshly peeled orange filled the room now. And paint. "I need to get area rugs." Her brain wanted to focus on something mundane. "The trim looks good. I like the way it repeats the trim on the wainscoting." Now she needed to find a way to fill the room.

"Danica. I can help with the furniture."

"No. I'm good." The skin pieces of an orange curled in a meticulous pile next to an empty soda bottle on a small table. Was that all he had for lunch? When he left here, who was going to make sure he ate?

Ignoring Reid, she went to the table and gathered the trash. That was an easy problem to fix. Reid? She had no idea what to do with him.

"Danica. Let me stay and help." He now stood behind her, just a feather's width away.

If she leaned back, she would feel his heartbeat.

His hand lightly touched her upper arm. His breath was soft across the back of her neck. "We can tell everyone the truth. I have the job at the ranch. I don't have to officially work here if it's going to cause a problem, but I can help in other ways."

The trash can was by the door. It wasn't that difficult to walk across the room. Just a few steps. Before she found the strength to walk away, Reid lowered his head. She could smell the oranges on his breath. He tilted his head and pushed a few loose strands of her hair back.

Was he going to kiss her? She stood still, not breathing. Waiting.

His lips were next to her ear, but he didn't touch her.

"I need to know how to make this right." His hands gently cupped her elbows. From there, they slipped down to her palms. Long fingers weaved between hers. "I don't know where to start, but the thought of leaving and never seeing..." His hands tightened around hers. "I want to help fill the pages of those photo albums. Whatever it takes to earn that privilege, please let me."

"Reid—" Her phone vibrated, and didn't stop. Someone was calling her. With one hand, she balanced the orange peels, or tried to anyway. A few pieces fell to the ground. With her free hand, she lifted the phone to her ear as she took a step forward, away from his warmth.

Staying close to her, he picked up the

fallen scraps and the ones still in her hands to dump them in the trash.

She was so distracted by him, she didn't understand a word Jackie said. "What?"

"You didn't return my text. What's going on?"

"It's fine. I told Reid about the replacement. He's leaving." She made the mistake of looking at him. Leaning against the doorframe, blocking her way out. He crossed his arms, and a grim expression set hard on his face.

"I'm on my way," Jackie practically yelled at her through the phone.

"Jackie, cut the drama. Really, you're overreacting. We were talking about the—"

Reid rushed past her to the window. Looking out, he muttered something about someone being out there. She couldn't understand. Just as fast, without explanation, he ran out the door.

"Danica! What is going on?" Jackie demanded her attention.

"Sorry. I have to go." Not bothering to listen to her sister, she ended the call and went looking for Reid. Instead, Bobby's truck cut in front of her. Everyone in her world was going crazy.

Engine still running, Bobby rolled down the window. "We got another hole in the fence. I don't think anyone got out this time, but you might want to get the Jeep and check out the north end of the property."

Dread filled her. Last night's board meeting had not gone well, but she'd reassured everyone she had it under control. *Lord, I need some major help here, on all fronts.*

"Have you seen Reid? We were talking, and he just ran out."

"Nope. Just came in to touch base with you and pick up some supplies. I won't be coming into the sanctuary tonight. Someone is sneaking around on our land in the dark, and I'm going to find them. So I'll be out there in the field if you need me."

"Who's doing this?" Hopelessness gripped her heart. She really couldn't do this much longer.

He shook his head and shifted gears. "Don't know. But we'll find them."

She stepped back so he could leave. Scanning the area for any sign of Reid, she made her way to the office. She wondered what could have happened. Had he gotten mad and left? He didn't have a car so he couldn't have gone back to the ranch. An ache in her belly started growing.

God, I need to turn this over to You. I'm stuck in the middle of a mess, and I don't know which way to go. You're my only way out.

Maybe if she'd trusted God more, she wouldn't be in this mess to begin with. *Forgive me. Guide me.* She wrapped her fingers around the braided leather bracelet on her left wrist. The charms she collected over time. Her favorite was the one her twin gave her when she first returned home, broken, pregnant and alone. John 16:33.

These things I have spoken to you, so that in Me you may have peace. In the world you have tribulation, but take courage; I have overcome the world.

A tiny laugh escaped her. The answer was always with her. Why did she ignore it until she became desperate?

As she started around the corner of the office, a horn blared from the road. A heavy sigh deflated her shoulders. Jackie had arrived. Great. More drama.

You have overcome the world, Lord. Please let me remember.

Dust flying, the green Suburban came to a stop at the front steps. Jackie had barely put it in Park before Sammi jumped out.

"Really, you brought reinforcements? You think Reid is that dangerous, or I'm that weak?"

Without permission, Sammi hugged her.

"I came for you. Jackie's always telling me what to do, too, so I thought you'd need backup."

Jackie shook her head as she joined them. "She thinks you'll do the smart thing. She didn't know about the dark place you went to last time he left."

"Maybe he's not leaving this time?" Sammi stood next to her and glared at Jackie.

"How did you become a hopeless romantic? Where did the optimism come from? It's unsettling."

Danica shook her head and started for the other side of the office. "Listen, I don't have time for personal issues right now. Bobby found another hole in the fence. Besides, Reid took off. I don't even know where he went."

Wrapping an arm around her waist, Sammi walked alongside her. "We'll go with you."

Jackie followed. "Another pair of eyes couldn't hurt. Do you know who's doing this?"

Danica sighed. "No, but Sheriff Torres is asking around."

"I hope he questions Reid. You do realize that it all started when he showed up."

"Ugh." Danica rolled her eyes but refused even to look at Jackie. "He has nothing to do with this."

"How do you know? It's a perfect setup for him to do an inside job."

Turning, she headed to the Jeep. "I don't have time for your crazy conspiracy theories. You watch too much TV. It rots the brain."

Sammi laughed. "It's been proven."

The bottom of Danica's stomach dropped. All four tires on the Jeep were flat. "That's not possible."

"They've been slashed." Jackie moved over to the four-wheelers. "These, too, and the trailer." Her sister looked at her. "Someone wanted to make sure you didn't get to the fences."

Sammi went down to look at them. "I

could change them, but I'd need tires. Do you have more than the one spare?"

All three sisters jumped when they heard a door slam. Reid rushed around the corner. He paused when he saw them, a short knife in his hands.

Jackie crossed her arms and glared at Reid. "Returning to the scene of the crime?"

That's all he needed right now, another hostile Bergmann. Reid sighed and tucked the knife back into the holder on his belt and focused on Danica. "Someone in a black hoodie was sneaking around the offices earlier." He glanced at the vehicles. Too late to do any good, and he didn't even find the person he'd been hunting. He looked at Jackie. "You think I did this?"

She shrugged. "Who else?"

"Whoever wants to make Danica look bad." Sammi stood next to Danica, her arm around her.

Reid nodded. "Someone doesn't want her

to get the grant. How close are you to getting the final word?"

The shrug was to give an I'm-not-worried vibe, but the concern in her eyes betrayed her. She was worried.

"They said the paperwork was in order. In a couple of weeks, they'll come for a visit." She scanned the vandalized property. "This is not good. I don't have the money to replace all these tires. I need to call Jake and let him know we've had more problems."

Reid checked the spare. "They didn't hit this one." He turned to Danica. She was on the phone with the sheriff, so he spun to face Sammi. The little sister seemed to be more welcoming at least. "Was Bobby here? Does he know about the tires? I know the ranch where I work keeps extra. Does she have some here?"

"I don't think so. Danica said Bobby was out checking fences, and she was going to join him. There are more holes."

Lifting his hat, he raked his fingers through

his hair. "I don't like this." A few strides around the Jeep to check it all out didn't give him any answers. There was no evidence screaming out the guilty person's name. "They didn't want us to get to the fences."

Jackie crossed her arms. "You disappear, then show up with a knife."

"I know I haven't done anything to prove you can trust me, but I'm here for one reason. To make things right. This is Danica's dream. I won't let anyone hurt it."

Danica joined them. "Jake will be here soon. He said not to touch anything."

He wanted to hold her but now wasn't the time. "I'll call Philip at the ranch. Maybe they can bring a couple of horses. We can ride the fences in the old-fashioned way."

Not looking at him, she nodded. "Okay. Thanks. I'm going inside to contact Bobby on the radio."

Catching up with her, he touched her elbow. "You know I didn't have anything to do with this, right? Jackie's way off base."

"I don't know what to think, other than someone wants me to fail." She took one step away from him, and he let her go. There wasn't anything else he could say.

Danica stopped and turned. "For what it's worth, I do believe you. I just don't have the energy to deal with anything else right now." She walked into the old bunkhouse, the screen door softly shutting behind her.

Reid pulled out his phone and started sending some text messages to the guys back at the ranch. There had to be something he could do to help. Hopefully, he had cavalry in his back pocket.

A black Mercedes pulled into the drive. Stephanie, the lawyer in high heels, got out and walked toward him. "I heard on the scanner that there's been trouble out here again." Even though she was much shorter, she managed to look down her nose at him. "What do you know about it?"

Danica opened the door and stepped onto

the porch. "Hi, Steph. I didn't expect to see you out here today."

"I'm worried that you've gotten in over your head. Have you thought about looking for alternatives for the animals? You don't want to be rushed if you have to close."

"We are not closing."

"I heard the big cats got out again." She made her way up the steps and put an arm around Danica to comfort her.

Reid wasn't buying it. "None of the animals have gotten out. Bobby found the holes in time, and I've got guys coming from the ranch with horses so we can check the rest of the fences."

Jackie and Sammi joined them. The glare he usually received was being shot at the lawyer now. Good, Jackie wasn't happy with her, either. "Danica has it under control. We don't need to be talking about shutting the place down. The sheriff will find out who's sabotaging the sanctuary, and she'll be back in business."

"Oh, I'm sure she'll be able to do it. I'm just worried about the stress and legal issues she is dealing with."

Reid lifted his head. "Legal issues?"

Danica stepped back, her forehead wrinkled. "What legal issues? Why didn't you say anything at the board meeting last night?"

"In a way, I did. I brought up the concern of having an ex-con working here. The neighboring ranchers are unhappy. With the lack of security and high rate of accidents, there are rumors of lawsuits." She sighed and put her hand on Danica's shoulder. "There's nothing concrete yet, so I didn't bring it up at the meeting, but I'm worried about you and what might happen."

Reid joined them on the porch. "I think a doomsday scenario is a little premature. The grant is looking good. Next week is the fund-raiser. I'm sure that will help." He looked at Danica. "You've got this."

He hated the doubt that clouded her eyes. Rumblings from the gate caused them all to turn. Two heavy-duty trucks were pulling in long gooseneck trailers, followed by another truck. Cowboys and horses from the Hausman ranch had arrived. More than he'd expected, and far more quickly than he'd hoped.

Nose in the air, the lawyer crossed her arms. "Who's that?"

Hopping down the steps, Reid turned back and grinned. "The cavalry."

Samantha let out a holler and ran up next to him. Her arm locked around his. She leaned in and whispered low. "You just might be hero material yet."

She ran ahead and greeted the men getting out of the trucks. The trailer came loaded with saddled horses, ready to ride. He glanced back at Danica. She smiled at him, then called out from the porch, "I'll get a few radios for them so they can connect with Bobby."

He grinned and turned back to greet the crowd of cowboys here to help, just because he'd asked. His chest swelled with humble gratitude. If only he could be that for Danica. He'd give anything to be her hero again, but time was running out.

Chapter Twelve

The church was quiet as Reid walked into the empty worship area. A week had passed since the last incident at the ranch, and no new information had surfaced. He couldn't help but notice some people were looking at him with suspicion. He wasn't sure if it was just who he was or if they thought he had something to do with the recent trouble at the wildlife refuge.

His boots didn't make a sound on the dark red carpet as he walked to the front of the church. At the steps, he fell to his knees. From his worn denim jacket, he pulled out the beat-up leather Bible. In his rough, calloused hands, it was small, but the words had changed his life.

During the second year of his sentence, Ray had invited him to a small group Bible study. He hadn't been interested, but it had been something to do, so he'd gone.

For the first time, he heard that God loved him, that he was worthy of that love. Not because of what he'd done, but because he was a child of God. Lost, but still wanted.

Grace was his, but now he struggled with his pride again. How did he differentiate God's plan from his desires?

Old yellow ribbons marked the verses he tried to live by in his new life. Philippians 3:13–14: *Brothers, I do not consider myself yet to have taken hold of it. But one thing I do: forgetting what is behind and straining toward what is ahead, I press on toward the goal to win the prize for which God has called me heavenward in Christ Jesus.*

It was easier to let go of the past in prison

when he couldn't see the consequences of his choices firsthand. He'd hurt Danica, and his daughters had been raised without a father.

He flipped to his second yellow ribbon. Revelation could be a dark and difficult book, but it had called to him. He touched the 2:10 verse. *Do not be afraid of what you are about to suffer. I tell you, the devil will put some of you in prison to test you, and you will suffer persecution for ten days. Be faithful, even to the point of death, and I will give you life as your victor's crown.*

Lowering his head, Reid prayed. He opened his heart and his mind to the word of God. It all seemed so murky. All he wanted was a clear path. Lifting his head, he studied the stained glass designs above the large painting behind the baptismal. The lamb lay at the base of the cross. A dove flew overhead.

"Lord, I come to You not knowing what to do. You know my heart. I love Danica and our daughters, but is leaving them the tribulation I have to walk through? Or do I stay and fight for them? I won't be welcomed by her family or the community. Is this my test? What is Your will?"

In the stillness, he waited, but nothing came. Silence echoed in his head. He bent forward, pressing his forearms against the polished wood that made the upper-level floor.

"Reid?" Pastor Levi stood behind the grand piano. "My secretary said you were looking for me. Do you still want to talk?"

"I don't mean to bother you." Checking the time, he sighed. "I just needed to talk to someone to get my head on straight before I saw Danica and the whole town at the rodeo tonight."

"It's no bother." Pastor Levi sat on the edge of the piano bench and leaned forward, resting his elbows on his knees. "What can I help you with?"

Reid licked his dry lips. How did he explain without telling him everything? "Will this be confidential, just between you and me?"

"If that's what you need. As long as it's not unlawful." He gave him a half smile like maybe he was joking, but maybe not.

"No, I'm not planning on breaking the law. That didn't work out so well for me last time." He shifted so he sat on the top step and looked at the side windows with all the colored glass. It was easier than looking straight at the pastor. "Danica and I eloped in college before I was locked up. We're married."

"Okay. So the girls are yours?"

"Yes." Claiming them made his heart burst with pride. To get to say they were his made him choke on unfamiliar emotions. He pressed his forehead hard into his palms. It also felt like he was betraying Danica. "She didn't want anyone to know. Even her family isn't aware we're married. They know the twins are mine, but that doesn't do much to endear me to them. She's embarrassed that she married me."

"That's got to be tough. What are you struggling with tonight?"

"She wants me to leave. I didn't know about the girls before I got here. I just wanted to make amends, apologize and move on, but she's still my wife. We have daughters. I want to respect her wishes, but I can't just walk out on them again. I don't know what to do. I want to submit to God's will, but it's hard to know what His will is. I keep waiting for His voice to tell me what to do, but I get nothing. Is there something wrong with me?"

"A burning bush would be nice, but it's not always that clear or easy. Sometimes we just don't see it. I do know that God's voice won't come in anger, fear, or doubt." He pointed to the opened Bible. "What are you reading?"

"Revelation 2:10."

He nodded. "That's a good one. I see why you're reading it. What does it mean to you?"

"Not living in fear. That's what got me in trouble the first time. I feared not having enough money. I feared that she would stop loving me. I didn't understand how she could love someone like me to begin with. So I reminded myself that choices made out of fear only lead to regret." A peace settled over him. "I have to take the fear out of the equation." He looked at the pastor. "That's easier said than done."

"Yeah. Living in fear can be a survival technique. So, ignoring that fear seems counterintuitive." Pastor Levi sat up and turned to face the piano. "Do you mind if I play? It helps me focus and think."

"No. I've always loved music. I tried learning to play, but I couldn't get past a few chords." The piano strings hummed a soft sweet tune, helping Reid relax.

"In your verse." The pastor kept his eyes on the keys and his fingers. The music filled the room. "It talks about prison. What do you think about that?"

"Prison is where I found God. In a way, it was so much easier there. I had a clear path. Now that I'm free, I thought I'd be happy. But I'm in a different kind of prison now. I'm more trapped than ever."

"What has you trapped?"

"This guilt. I abandoned Danica when she needed me most. How can I even ask for forgiveness? She made it clear from day one not to expect anything from her, and I don't blame her, but I want to be a father to my girls. The Bible talks about the sins of the father. I thought I could be better, I tried. None of the men in my family ever graduated high school. I wanted to break those chains, but I panicked and tried for the easy money, not only destroying my future but letting down Danica and leaving my girls without a father. Just like my dad."

"One mistake doesn't have to shape your whole future. You can make the decision that your past will not become your future. Of course, the one thing you can't control is

Danica. It's up to her if you get to be back in her life." He stopped playing and turned to Reid. "It takes time to rebuild trust. Once it's been destroyed, it won't be easily given again. What are the alternatives? What about you staying close and being part of her life indirectly?"

"That's what I've offered, but I don't know if I can watch the girls without being their father. Or maybe that's the trial I have to walk through. Plus, I don't know how much longer we can really keep pretending they aren't mine. We have the same eyes, and I think the sheriff has noticed. He probably thinks I'm a deadbeat dad."

"Living with secrets is never healthy." The pastor picked up the beat, then let it fade away into a slow melody. "The longer you don't tell the truth, the harder it gets. Is there a reason she doesn't want anyone to know?"

"Fear? I don't know other than she didn't believe I would stick around long."

"You've been here for a few months now. Any plans to leave?"

"No. I'd like to make it my home if she'd let me."

"Have you told her that?"

"I figured she knew that by now."

"You want her to just know your intentions? It helps if we talk to people, and don't assume they know. It creates a lot of problems. Believe me, I know that firsthand."

"Tonight, after the rodeo, I need to make time to have a heart-to-heart. What if she doesn't want me here?"

"You're not who you used to be. You're redeemed, and you need to let her know what your wants and fears are. If the girls are important to you, you need to let her know you are willing to do whatever it takes to be their father. She might need more than words. The past can be hard to overcome."

"Yes, but it's worth fighting the fight. If this is what I have to do, then I can be a patient man. I hope she hears me."

The pastor stood from the bench and joined him on the steps. "You want to pray before you leave?"

"Yeah, I'd like that. I feel like my whole life is riding on this one conversation."

"It's not. Just take a deep breath, and have faith."

Reid laughed. "Isn't there a warning about praying for patience?"

Pastor Levi put his hand on Reid's shoulder. "Yes, sir. Let's pray."

They bowed their heads, and Reid let the words of the pastor's prayer wash over him. It was cleansing.

Now to face Danica and the whole town. Would he ever get to stand with his family in public? He couldn't help but feel tonight his life was going to take a new direction, hopefully one that involved Danica and their daughters.

The dust and sounds of a rodeo created a familiar chaos that Danica usually loved, but tonight Reid was riding a bull. If he showed up. She scanned the grounds for Reid. He was always early to anything he went to, even back in college. Maybe he'd changed his mind and wasn't coming. Her breath caught in her throat.

Maybe he had finally decided to leave. He wasn't happy when she told him about the new vet tech. The thought that he would leave for good hit her hard. She wasn't sure how she felt about it, but it wasn't good.

Everyone eventually left anyway, so she didn't know why she was so surprised. Some of the cowboys waved as they walked past her. She made sure to smile, but inside she wanted to curl up under her covers and hide. He must have left.

She'd almost told the girls who he was, but now they didn't have to know that their father walked out on them again. Why had she expected anything different?

"Because you're a pathetic dreamer who never learns your lesson." She pulled herself up on the railing. She needed to find something to distract herself with or she was going to cry.

"I don't know what lesson you're working on, but you've never come close to being pathetic."

She jumped at the sound of Reid's voice. His hands went to her waist to steady her. She glared over her shoulder.

He laughed. "Didn't mean to scare you. Dani girl, you're one of the smartest people I know. If there's something you need to learn, I have no doubt you'll master it."

"You're late." Danger lurked in those gray twinkling eyes, so she turned to break the line connecting them. Staring straight ahead, she really couldn't say what she was looking at. He was just inches away.

"Watching for me were you, baby?" He stepped up to the railing next to her and leaned over, resting his chin on his forearms. He watched the same arena she did.

"No. They're pulling the bulls soon. If you're late, you'd forfeit your ride and entry fee."

"Yeah, I remember how it works. Looks like a great turnout."

"People around here are good at supporting the local nonprofits. It's not just us, but the volunteer fire department and the youth center."

"The funds should help hold you over until you get the grant."

"I hope so, as long as we don't suffer any more problems. I'm sick to my stomach at the idea that someone wants us to fail."

"It doesn't make sense. The ranchers are more of the straightforward type. What happens to the property if the sanctuary fails?"

"If I have to close the doors in the next couple of years, it reverts back to Linda's estate, but the only family left is Stephanie."

"Really?" He turned his full attention on her. "How much is the land worth? You don't think that would be motive enough, do you?"

"No. She doesn't want the ranch, so I'm

hoping to work out a deal with her if it comes down to that. So don't go there. She's been my strongest advocate since Linda's death. I don't know what I would have done without her advice and support."

"She's made it clear she doesn't like—" He tucked his head. "You're right. I don't know her enough to make judgments. I just don't think this is the ranchers' style of fighting."

"Which takes us right back where we started. With nothing."

"Tonight, I want some time to talk to you. Just the two of us. No interruptions."

Her stomach dipped. "Is everything all right?" The announcer called the bull riders to the back gate. "You better go. We'll talk tonight. I'll have Jackie take the girls home."

He nodded as he hopped from the railing. Pausing, he stared at her. For a moment, she thought he might move in for a kiss. It seemed too natural. Swallowing, she hooked one arm over the rail. "Be safe. Don't wrap your hand in. You don't do that anymore, do you?"

"No, ma'am. I'll be ready to jump clear when I'm done."

"You're getting too old for this, you know. A father has to make sure he's whole and healthy for his children's sake. You need to start thinking about that kind of thing."

His grin grew wider as if she'd given him a gift he'd always wanted.

"Duly noted. So, let's say this is my last ride." He took a step closer. "I have no problem walking away from the bulls if I'm walking to you and the girls."

She wasn't sure how it happened, but the world shifted, and she leaned forward to touch her lips to his. Just for a moment. Then she remembered where she was and pulled back, glancing around. What had she just done?

Hands in his pockets, he stepped back. "Don't panic. I don't think anyone saw you kiss the convict."

The hurt in his eyes tore at her heart. "Reid."

"No worries. I've got to go. But before I forget, I have your keys. The Jeep was blocking a gate, so I moved it for the guys. You shouldn't leave them in an unlocked car."

"I should lock them in the car?" She smiled at his eye roll. "I trust everyone around here. These are hometown people."

"You never really know what hidden agendas they might have." He pulled the keys out of his pocket and looked at the preschool pictures she had on the chain.

She held out her hand, but he slipped them back into his jeans.

"I think I'll keep them for now. After the rodeo, we can drive somewhere to talk."

All she could manage was a nod. Their relationship would take another turn tonight; she could feel it. For good or bad, they would have to make a decision about the future. Her stomach was in a knot. What direction were they going? She hated the unknown.

She watched him until he was out of eyesight. Then she climbed up as high as she could on the railing, scanning the back of the gates to try and find him. What did he want to talk about?

"I'm thinking you two have more of a past than you let on."

"Jake!" One hand went to her chest. "You startled me. Sorry, I mean Sheriff Torres."

"Stop that. You've known me too long to not call me Jake. Are the girls running tonight?"

"No, I don't think they're old enough yet for the type of speed that will be needed for this event."

He nodded and adjusted his tan cowboy hat. "So, I've been digging around and found your latest volunteer was in the same program at A&M the exact same time you were. On the rodeo team, too. He went to prison about the time you came home pregnant."

"What does this have to do with the investigation?"

"I need all the facts to make sure I have

everything I need to put the puzzle together. Everyone always comments on the unusual eye color of the twins." He stopped talking and just stared at her.

Scanning the arena, she found the girls with Jackie and her dad in the stands. "It's a personal issue that we're working out. I'd rather do it without any drama. He has nothing to do with the accidents."

"A couple of the board members disagree. They think the problems started when he showed up, and your judgment is impaired when it comes to him."

"What? That's ridiculous. He stayed so we could get the certification." She took a deep breath. "He has nothing to do with the problems."

"There's also some concern that you're desperate and willing to make some questionable decisions."

"I'm sorry, Sheriff Torres, but this is sounding like you're questioning me in the investigation."

"Just a friendly chat, trying to get the whole picture."

"If you have any more questions, please make it official. Maybe I should talk to my lawyer."

"If that's what you feel you need to do."

"Thank you for being here tonight. I'm going to find my girls to watch the rest of the rodeo. Good night."

"'Night, Danica."

She was well aware that he was watching her walk away. She wanted to run and find Reid. People were talking about them. Already questioning his relationship with the girls. She should have been better prepared.

But what was she doing? Kissing him. Ugh. She hit the side of her head. Stupid.

"Momma! Did you see Mia's run!" Lizzy jumped with excitement.

"It was awesome. Please let me ride next year!" Suzie wasn't going to give up her desire to ride at a higher level.

"Look what Aunt Jackie did." Glad Lizzy

was changing the subject, Danica let her girls pull her forward to Jackie and her father. They were her world and everything she did would affect them.

"She has the camera Mr. Reid put on the baby bats!"

"Look!" Suzie held Jackie's phone up.

Right now, she needed to be with the girls. They deserved all her attention. Jackie looked at her with a question in her eyes. Taking a deep breath, she smiled, shook her head and looked at the phone screen. The time with her family was the most important.

"I see Mr. Reid!" Suzie stood and waved. "Mr. Reid!"

Not to be outdone Lizzy joined her sister and yelled his name, too.

"Girls, sit down." Leaning in, she kept her voice low. Glancing up, she saw Reid waving back, a big grin on his face. Her heart skipped a beat. He walked along the catwalk behind the chutes. Lean muscles moved over his frame as fluidly as the river moved over the rocks, smooth and easy. Back in college, she'd had a hard time keeping her gaze away from him. Now he was even more interesting. Not the boy anymore, but a man.

Jackie looped her arm around Danica's. "One thing I can say for sure, you picked one good-looking man."

"He has a good heart, too. If you take the time to get to know him. He had a hard life."

"Don't blame me. He's the one that left you. Got stuck in prison. And he didn't even bother to tell you." She pressed her head to Danica's. "Don't get blinded by those beautiful eyes of his. You deserve someone that will be by your side and stay there no matter what. No one is going to hurt my little sister again."

"You're only older by five minutes," Danica said out of habit. Reid was good-looking, but it was so much more than his charm that captured her heart. "What if he's changed? Do you believe in redemption and second chances?"

"Not if my sister and nieces are the ones who were hurt."

"Hey, guys. Sammi's running next." Nikki slid into the bench seat behind them. Adrian was holding her hand.

Her father patted Adrian on the back. "Mia had a good run."

With a father's pride, he nodded. "Yeah, it was her best time. Don't think it will keep her in the top five, but each run has gotten faster."

"Did you hear which bull Reid pulled?" Danica couldn't even pretend not to care.

Adrian laughed. "He pulled Mr. Darcy."

Her forehead wrinkled. "The bull's name is Mr. Darcy? That doesn't sound very tough."

"No, and the bull must be mad about it. He wants to charge every cowboy he sees. I don't think anyone has stayed on him for a full eight yet. He's a tough one."

All the color must have left her face, because Nikki elbowed her husband.

"Oh, sorry. Reid seems to be the type to handle himself well."

When they were younger, she loved watching him ride. The adrenaline was a rush, and to think he was hers was exciting. Now all she saw were the ways he could get hurt or killed. Those bulls were two thousand pounds of muscles, hooves and horns.

"He'll be fine." Adrian smiled and tried to reassure her again.

Her father pointed to the gate. "Samantha's about to run."

The girls started cheering. "Go, Aunt Sammi!"

Sammi and her roan mare charged into the arena, cutting so close to the first barrel it wobbled, but it ultimately stayed in place. Finishing all three barrels, she lay over her horse's neck and sprinted home. The announcer called her time. It was the best of the night. They all stood and cheered.

A truck drove out into the arena and hauled the barrels away, clearing the deep sand for the last event. The bull riding. Danica's stomach clinched. She wasn't sure she could even watch.

Her family kept up a constant stream of conversation, and she let them distract her. She loved them for it. Then it was Reid's turn. The girls got excited seeing him climb into the chute as they got the bull ready.

Eight seconds. That was all, then it would be over. Knots pulled her insides tight, twisting beyond her stomach and squeezing her heart. It was easier to look elsewhere. That's when she noticed a couple of unfamiliar cars pull into the area behind the gates.

Men in suits got out, and Sheriff Torres walked over to them. Shaking hands, they talked.

A whole new fear took all the energy out of her muscles, and a nauseating numbness took over. Was Reid in trouble? It couldn't be him. He hadn't done anything.

James joined them. A sweat broke out over her entire body, despite the breeze. His parole officer was involved?

James had other jobs in the county so it might have nothing to do with Reid. It was just a coincidence they were all together where Reid was about to ride.

She glanced over at him. He nodded with his arm high in the air. She wanted to yell at him. To warn him. About what, she wasn't sure.

The gate swung open. The bull came out spinning. The crowd went crazy as the big animal changed directions, but Reid moved with him. Leaning back, then coming forward, his movements rolled with the bull. The horns thrust at the air as the bull kicked and twisted. Eight seconds had never lasted so long.

At one point, she stood but didn't remember moving. The twins were jumping up and down. Finally, the buzzer went off, but the ride wasn't over. He still had to dismount and clear the arena without getting gored or stepped on. The rodeo clowns moved in to distract the dangerous animal as Reid jumped from his back. He was thrown with such force that he landed on his knees in the deep sand.

Danica gripped Adrian's arm as Mr. Darcy lowered his head and ran at Reid.

The shorter clown darted between them and waved a flag. Another came up behind to get the bull's attention. Reid was on his feet and ran for the railing closest to him. Which was where she and her family sat. With a jump, he climbed up and waved his hat to let the crowd know he was good. Just a few feet from them, he tossed the girls his hat, a huge grin on his face.

Adrian whistled. "That was a great ride. It has to be in the nineties."

Reid jumped from the rail and thanked the cowboys as the bull now went calmly into the back gate. The girls fought over who got to wear the hat. All Danica wanted to do was grab him and make sure he was whole and healthy. She didn't trust that smile. He was good at hiding bruises. Once he even walked off with a smile with a busted rib.

She leaned in to tell Jackie she was going to check on him. With a small eye roll, her sister nodded. At least they had gotten past lecturing. Halfway down the steps, law officers met her. Jake and James looked grim.

She didn't recognize the other men with them. This couldn't be good. "James. Jake." She nodded at them, then glanced at the men with them. "Is there a problem?"

One of the men handed her a sheet of paper. "Do you recognize the narcotics listed here?"

Nodding, she looked up at the men. "Sure. These are some of the drugs we keep on the sanctuary."

"Do you currently have any in your possession, or do you know of any missing in your inventory?"

"No. Why would I—"

James moved closer to her. "There's been an anonymous report—"

The tall stranger with dark aviators stepped forward. "Officer, we'll take care of this. Mrs. Bergmann, we need to check a Jeep that belongs to the Hill Country Wildlife Rescue."

"The Jeep is here, but I don't understand." She looked at Torres. "Is this about our conversation earlier?"

"What's going on?" Reid came up behind her. His hand rested on her lower back.

The simple touch calmed her. "They want to check the Jeep."

He looked at the sheriff. "Do you have a warrant?"

"We were hoping she would make this easy and work with us."

Reid started to say something else, but she placed a hand on his arm. "It's fine." She moved around the men and marched in the direction of her car. They all turned and followed her. She stopped when she realized it wasn't where she'd left it.

Her heart froze. Reid had moved the Jeep. She didn't know where it was parked now. She looked at him. A nasty feeling paralyzed her. The last thing he needed was to be involved in any type of investigation with drugs.

Jake walked up next to her. "What's wrong?"

"Um. Forgot where I parked." Not wanting to say anything else, she glanced at Reid.

"Oh, I moved it." He dug into his pocket. "Here are the keys."

"Do you have access to all company vehicles?" one of the suits asked.

James cleared his throat. "Let's just go to the car. We'll ask the questions that need to be answered then."

The small group followed Reid to the back of the dirt parking lot, weaving through the maze of trucks and trailers. When they reached the Jeep, one of the unknown law officers asked them to unlock the car. As soon as the click was heard, they started searching. Even though she knew there was nothing for them to find, fear gripped her.

"Mr. Reid!" Suzie yelled as she and Lizzy ran toward them, followed by the rest of Danica's family.

Chapter Thirteen

Reid was having a hard time breathing. He was surrounded by law officers searching Danica's car, and now her family ran to them. Suzie had his black cowboy hat on. The smile on her face became his whole world for a moment.

He went down, and she ran to him. "I get to wear your hat first, then Lizzy gets it. Opa said we have to give it back to you, though."

"I gave it to y'all. If you want it, you get to keep it."

"Thank you." She hugged him.

"Now you have to promise to share it."

Lizzy was right next to her. "It's my turn to wear it."

"Girls, not now. I'll hold it if you start fighting."

"Yes, ma'am," they said in stereo. Lizzy leaned in and whispered something to her sister, and the hat was handed over.

Mr. Bergmann frowned at the sheriff. "Why are there men searching my daughter's car." He glanced at Reid like it was somehow his fault.

"Something to do with the drugs that are kept at the wildlife refuge."

Deep lines creased her father's forehead. "Drugs?"

Jackie approached the sheriff. "Jake, this is ridiculous. You know Danica. She wouldn't do anything illegal."

Reid's instinct was to run, but there wasn't a reason. Everything he did when he returned was to stay out of trouble. But they had the power to take away his freedom, his life. His father's shadow was long and dark.

James shook his head. "Not our call, but we'll have it cleared up soon."

The men turned, one holding up baggies full of drugs that had been locked in the medicine cabinet at the sanctuary yesterday. The other man pulled out a bank bag. It was the one from the concession stand. Cash was stuffed inside.

Reid couldn't breathe. This had to be a nightmare.

"Mrs. Bergmann, do you recognize these?"

"Of course. It's a drug we use on our big animals. We keep them locked up, so I don't know why they are in the trunk of my car. That money isn't mine. I don't keep money in my trunk."

"And these. Are you claiming you have no knowledge of these, either?" With a horse blanket pulled back, there seemed to be hundreds of small baggies of white powder.

His knees turned to mush.

Danica looked confused. "What is that?"

Without a doubt, Reid knew that they

were in trouble. Someone was about to be arrested, and they were not looking at him. The tall officer took Danica by the arm. Handcuffs out, he started reciting the Miranda rights.

"No!" He couldn't let them put those on her. He stepped between them, blocking her from the man's touch. "It's mine. She doesn't even know what that is."

"Reid?" She twisted around to look at him. "What's going on?"

The sheriff was called over the radio on the man's shoulder. He stepped away, and everyone turned to stare at Reid. "Who are you?" the one with the aviators asked.

James sighed. "He's my parolee. Reid McAllister."

"What was he in for?"

"Drug trafficking."

"And you had full access to this car?"

"I had the keys. I was the last one to drive it." There was no way he was going to let them put Danica in handcuffs.

James nodded, his expression grim. "He's the vet tech at the sanctuary. He has full access to the drugs."

The disappointment in his parole officer's eyes was hard to take. Unable to make eye contact with anyone, Reid kept his focus on the distant hills. He was commanded to turn around and put his hands flat on the car. He locked his jaw to keep the bile down as they searched him.

"What are you doing?" Danica's voice was unusually high. "Reid hasn't done anything wrong. He has nothing to do with this."

He cut a hard glare right at her. "Take the girls and leave." He couldn't even glance at the girls who were so happy to see him just a minute ago.

"What's wrong? What's happening?" The girls' voices mingled. He squeezed his eyes shut. Blocking out the world, he closed down all emotions and thoughts. What had he just done?

"Jackie. Sammi. Take the girls." Mr. Bergmann's voice was firm but edged with anger.

Reid dared to glance over his shoulder. Sammi was holding Lizzy, and Jackie had Suzie as they rushed from the scene. Away from him.

They pulled his arms behind him, locking them down tighter than was probably necessary. Danica still stood next to him. He couldn't look at her. "Go, Danica."

"Reid, no. You didn't do this. Tell them you didn't do this."

He growled. Why was she so stubborn? "Go!" He lowered his voice. "I don't want you here."

She touched James's arm. "He didn't do this. I don't know who did this, but it wasn't Reid."

"This doesn't look good, Danica. I suggest you leave with your father. The car will be compounded for evidence."

"Reid?" Her voice broke.

He couldn't afford to look at her.

This was it. It was over. He had hoped he could be a new man in Christ, but handcuffs were back, and this time he hadn't even done anything wrong.

"Daddy, do something." Danica wasn't leaving.

He hated the desperation he heard in her voice. Arms locked in place behind him, Reid stared at the horizon over the top of the Jeep. The tall officer listed his rights, but he'd heard it all before.

Danica shot forward. "No! He didn't do this. He's just—"

"Danica." Reid's voice was sharper and angrier than he'd intended, but they would arrest her if they thought she was going to cause problems. "Stop it. Go with your father. The girls need you."

Her father grabbed her arm and started pulling her away. She called out to him. "Don't say anything. Do you hear me, Reid McAllister? Don't speak another word. I'll get a lawyer. We'll figure this out."

They pushed him forward, back to their car. "Leave," he growled through locked jaws.

Her father finally got her out of the way. Good. Making this walk alone was better. It was.

People gawked. Speculated. Whispered. The grounds seemed unnaturally quiet. How did he think he could belong with the respectable people of this community? Head down, he was tucked into the back seat. The door slammed.

He stared straight ahead. If he made eye contact with anyone here that he had come to think of as a friend, he'd lose it.

A black void crept into the edges of his vision. Drugs. He'd admitted to stealing and transporting drugs. Prison again. And this time, they wouldn't let him out. He'd be locked away forever. It was over. *God, I don't understand. I just don't understand.*

The handcuffs cut into his wrists as he instinctively strained against them. For the first time in his messed-up adult life, he wanted to yell and sob. Head down, he stayed silent.

Chapter Fourteen

Danica and her dad caught up to Jackie as she got done settling the girls into the back seat of the Suburban. "Daddy, we have to get him out. He didn't do it."

Her father shut the car door and glared at her. "How do you know? He's been in prison for transporting drugs before. He's from the streets. This is what I was worried about when you brought him home six years ago."

"He hadn't done anything six years ago until he wanted to make enough money to impress you. But we aren't talking about six years ago. Today they came to arrest me.

They came for me! Someone claimed that I was stealing drugs and selling them from the trunk of my car. When he saw them, Reid came over to help me. If it were his stuff, he would have taken off. He didn't know it was there any more than I did."

He turned on her, his face hard and unforgiving. "So why did he claim it was his?"

She hadn't seen him this angry in a long time. "To protect me. He didn't do this. I just know it."

Jackie came around from the other side and put her arm around Danica. "I'm not a fan of his, but even I can tell he did this for her. He didn't want her to get arrested, so he said it was his. Words mean nothing, but his actions today showed me his character." Pressing her forehead to Danica's, Jackie's eyes glistened with moisture. "Daddy, don't you see? He sacrificed his freedom, to take her place."

"Then who did it?" Now her father just looked confused.

"I don't know. Someone that had access to the sanctuary and wants it to fail." It had to be someone she knew, and that was just too hard to imagine. "They set me up to get arrested. Whoever is damaging the fences did this. They're sabotaging any chance of us getting the certification and the grant."

Her father looked over her shoulder. "He took your place?"

"Yes. Reid allowed them to put him in cuffs to protect me. I can't let him go it alone. I need bail, and a lawyer I can trust."

"We can help with bail." Nikki walked up with Adrian.

He nodded. "Whatever you need, we're here."

"Thank you!" She hugged each of them, holding them tight.

"What about Stephanie?" Her father crossed his arms. "Can she help?"

"She's on the board, and I can't go there for help with personal issues. Plus, Reid doesn't trust her." She pressed her palm against her stomach. Who could she trust? Her world was upside down. "I'm not sure I do, either. I'm not allowing Reid to fight this alone. I'll get him out."

Her family deserved the whole truth. Secrets had to end. "There is something that I never told you." She glanced at the girls tucked safely in the back seat. The rest of her family stared at her, waiting. "In college… during Spring Break, Reid and I eloped. We're married."

Her father turned and hit the hood of the car. "I told him no!"

"We shouldn't have kept it a secret, but I wouldn't change anything." She glanced at the girls, now wide-eyed and looking more worried than before. "He's made mistakes, but he didn't do this. I can't let him take the fall for something he didn't do."

Jackie nodded and put her hand on her father's arm. "Right now, we need to stay focused on the main problem. We'll start with bail."

"I'll cover bail." Her father turned when he spoke, startling everyone into silence. He approached Danica and cupped her cheek. "What did I do to make my girls think they had to hide so much from me?"

She shook her head, eyes burning. "I didn't want to hurt or disappoint you. When he left, I was too embarrassed to tell anyone." She glanced at her sister. For the first time ever, she couldn't tell what Jackie was thinking.

Her father grunted. "There's a lot to talk about, but right now we need to get the girls home. I'll call Sonia. I'm sure she'll watch them so we can get him out."

"We're coming, too." Nikki looked at Adrian.

He nodded. "I'll take Mia home to George. We'll get Sammi and her horse, and be right behind you."

"Then let's meet at the house and make a plan. Does anyone know how much bail will be?"

"I'll call James." Danica held her phone

up to her ear as they all climbed into the Suburban. She had told her family the truth, and they were still there. In the back seat, the twins were unusually quiet. Leaving a message for James, she turned to them. "Are you okay?"

They nodded, talking around each other at the same time. "Momma, why did they take Mr. Reid away? Did he do something to get in trouble again? Is Opa mad at us for being nice to him?"

Her whole world shrank, crushing her beneath a sudden pressure. She glanced at her father, his jaw clenching. She could barely speak, her voice shaky. "No, sweetheart. Of course not." She looked them both in the eye. "Reid isn't in trouble. It's just a mistake, and we are going to straighten it out."

Her father put the monster in Drive and weaved through the parking lot, people staring. She wasn't going to hide her husband any longer.

They were about to pull out of the fairgrounds when Cody Baxter, the foreman of the Hausman ranch, stopped them. She rolled down her window. "Do you need something, Cody?"

"One of my wranglers was just escorted out in handcuffs. You know what's going on?"

"He didn't do anything wrong. We're going now to bail him out and get this fixed."

He adjusted his hat. "Let me know what we can do to help. Wouldn't be the first good cowboy working for me that had a mix-up with the law."

"Thank you. I'm sure he'll be back to work as soon as we get him out." They nodded at each other, and he walked away.

Now she needed to tell the girls, but maybe that was something they'd do together. She just needed to get him out first.

Reid wasn't sure he heard correctly when they told him he'd made bail. "You have the wrong guy. I'm Reid McAllister."

They looked at him as if he was a little off, but ignored him and went through the process. He was being released. It didn't make any sense. Who would do that for him?

There hadn't been anyone to call. Maybe the guys he worked with at the ranch? Cowboys could be a close group, but he hadn't been there long enough to gain bail money loyalty.

Did he even have a job anymore? Employers definitely frown on drug dealers who steal money from a fund-raiser. That was just about the lowest.

There was Danica. She hadn't turned away from him at the time of the arrest, but she didn't have that kind of money or collateral to make bail. If she even would.

He swallowed back emotion, remembering how she'd argued with the police. No one had ever fought for him before.

Last time he'd been arrested, he just stayed in jail. When he got out, Ray was going to pick him up, but his wife had gone into early labor. So he couldn't blame the guy for that one. Being alone was nothing new.

That night he had walked past huge signs on the road, warning drivers they were close to a prison and shouldn't pick up hitchhikers. He hadn't really minded walking the miles to the bus stop that took him to Kerrville, though. For the first time in six years, there hadn't been a fence or someone telling him where to go.

Tonight, however, there were no buses. Maybe he could call Pastor Levi, but it was too late. He glanced at his watch. Or too early.

Man, if he didn't have a job, he didn't have a place to live. He needed to let James know he was out at least. Opening the heavy door at the end of the hall, he looked up from the dull, worn tiles and froze.

Danica walked toward him, then paused. The ugly green chairs were filled with people he recognized. They all stood, surrounding her like a small army of family and friends.

They were smart enough to not allow her to come alone.

He glanced behind him. Maybe it was safer back there with the bars between him and her support team. Like an idiot, he didn't move. Not knowing what to do, he rammed his fists into the pockets of his Levi's jacket. Why was she here?

He must have stood there too long, because she started moving toward him again. Taking a step back, he glanced over her shoulder at the grim faces behind her. They couldn't be happy she was here. "What are you doing, Danica? Where are the girls?"

"They're at the house with Sonia. We're here to take you home, and make sure you never come back. Why would you let them arrest you?" Her eyes cut all the way to his core, down to the soft spots he hid from the world.

How did he explain to her that she was

purity and innocence to him? She needed to be protected at all costs. "I couldn't let them put you in handcuffs. I'd do anything to keep you safe." The ugliness of his world couldn't touch her. It was bad enough he was in her life.

Mr. Bergmann walked up to him and held out his hand. Confused, Reid took it. The grip was firm. "Thank you, son."

Staring down at their hands, Reid couldn't quite get his thoughts lined up. *Son.* This couldn't be real.

Jackie stood on the other side of Danica. Clearing her throat, she crossed her arms and narrowed her eyes. "Someone wants the sanctuary to implode, and they set her up. You took the fall for her. For now, you're family. We need to get this figured out. So, what do we do now?"

Danica put her hand on his shoulder and looked into his eyes as if checking to see if he had a concussion. "I'm sure you need to eat." She looked at her crew. "We can go to that twenty-four-hour pancake place. There, we can make a game plan." Coming back to him, she paused. "Is that okay?"

The word *family* had stopped all brain function between his ears. He scanned the group. Nikki, Adrian, and Sammi, even Jackie and Mr. Bergmann were all here for him. Joaquin gave him a nod.

Not once in his life could he recall people being there for him. If he tried to utter a word, he might actually cry. He blinked and focused on Danica. Somehow, he managed a nod.

As the Bergmann herd turned and headed through the door, James greeted them. Reid's instinct was to run. He was out. Fresh air hit him as his boots stepped onto the sidewalk. Every fiber of his being rebelled at the thought of going back inside.

Breathe in, five...four...three...two...one. Breathe out.

James smiled. "Oh, good. You have a ride." He chuckled as he patted Adrian's shoulder. "More than one from the looks of it." He walked up to Reid and held out his hand. "Danica is convinced you had nothing to do with this and were just keeping her out of jail." He held his hand a little tighter when they shook and locked him in with eye contact. Then he nodded and backed up. "If you need anything, call me. Anytime."

Danica hugged him. "We will. Thank you, James."

He gave her a lopsided grin. "You should have told me I was asking a married woman out. I would have given up a lot sooner." With a tap to his cowboy hat, he left.

Married? They knew? They piled into the giant green Suburban. Danica opened the front passenger door for him. "Go ahead and ride up here with Daddy. I know how you feel about small spaces."

"They know we're married?"

"No more secrets. The girls are the only ones who don't know, but right now, we need to figure a way to keep you out of jail.

We'll talk to them later. Go on, get in before Sammi calls shotgun."

"Okay. Later." The idea that she not only knew about his problem with crowded seating but that she also cared just about undid him. He didn't deserve her. It had to be some fluke that she'd agreed to marry him six years ago, and now they were in the same place again.

What's the plan, God? Because I'm in way over my head. I have nothing left. Maybe this was where God wanted him. Paul had done ministry from prison. It wasn't the life he wanted, but he feared it was the life God intended for him.

Driving down the old highway, Mr. Bergmann glanced over at him. "You haven't said a word. What are you thinking?"

Reid didn't want to even try to put his thoughts into words, but Mr. Bergmann had offered a truce and deserved his respect. "I've heard people say God doesn't give us more than we can handle." Facing forward, he watched the lines on the highway. "But I think we get more than we can handle all the time. The trick is learning to trust God for strength and—"

He had to swallow. A hard knot clogged his throat. He wasn't saying it right. "I need to learn to let others help me. It's hard to let people see you when you're—" he looked out the side window "—not in a place of strength. I don't deserve your help."

"My daughter thinks you do. You protected her." He reached up, pulled an index card from his visor and handed it to Reid. "With all the girls in my house, I started using my car for prayer time years ago. I keep a couple of verses here. It seems appropriate for both of us to remember."

Written across the top in pencil was the verse 2 Corinthians 12:10. The last line went straight to his heart. *For Christ; for whenever I am infirm, then I am powerful.*

He looked at the man sitting next to him. The man who'd raised the woman Reid loved. "Raising four daughters alone had to take a great deal of faith and strength."

Gray eyebrows went up as he looked in the rearview mirror. Women's voices talked over each other, filling the vehicle. He shook his head. "I should have used more faith. I built walls and tried to control things I couldn't control. I made huge mistakes, and my girls paid the price."

Danica leaned across the bench seat in front of her. "Daddy, what are y'all talking about?"

"Daughters." Mr. Bergmann winked into the rearview mirror.

She rolled her eyes. After Mr. Bergmann had parked in front of the old corner drive, everyone climbed out. Thankfully, the restaurant was empty. They scooted into a large round corner booth, and orders were soon placed.

The sisters spoke all at once. Reid couldn't keep up with the threads of conversations.

They only paused when the drinks were sat on the table.

Adrian interjected, and they all went quiet. "None of that will matter if we don't find out who actually set Danica up. Who knew where all the drugs were kept and was also at the rodeo? They took that money out of the concession stand."

Silence settled over the group as they all turned inward. Reid hated his gut instinct. Danica wasn't going to like it. "I think we need to look at the lawyer, Stephanie. She has the most to gain if the sanctuary is closed."

Danica shook her head. "She doesn't want the land. But it doesn't matter. She wasn't at the rodeo."

Adrian frowned. "Yes, she was. I had spoken to her right before I left to join y'all in the stands. She told me she was worried the committee was wasting money by giving some of the earnings to Danica's rescue efforts. I thought she was just being a lawyer and looking at the negatives."

Playing with her straw, Danica kept her head down. "I don't want to believe it, but even if it were true, how would we even prove it?"

Everyone stopped talking as the smiling waitress loaded their table with pancakes, bacon, eggs and hash browns. Joaquin was the first to grumble something. "If only we had enough money for a security system at the sanctuary. We'd be able to catch whoever stole those drugs."

Reid cut into the tall stack of syrup-drenched pancakes, then froze. "The bats!"

Everyone looked at him as if he'd lost the last bit of his brain, but Danica sat straight up, her eyes wide. "The camera you installed. You can see the locked cabinets."

"There should be a seventy-four-hour backup. We need to get to the hard drive."

Jackie pulled her phone out. "I'll call

Vickie and see where Jake is. He can get the recordings and give it to the right people."

Samantha stood and waved down the waitress. "We need to-go boxes."

"I'll take care of the check." Mr. Bergmann moved to the register by the front door. "Tell Jake we'll be there in under an hour."

The trip was a blur. They all ate on the way, talking over each other. The Styrofoam box in his lap was empty, but he didn't remember eating a bite.

Jake's car, his parole officer's car and one he didn't recognize were parked in front of the bunkhouse.

Everyone climbed out and headed inside, but he found his body didn't want to move. Was it really going to be this easy? Nothing in his life ever worked out the way he wanted. His door opened.

Danica stood there. "What's wrong?" She took a step closer and placed her hand on his arm. "They aren't here to arrest you. We're going to find out who did this and the right person will go to jail."

"Why did you do this? Bailing me out. Trying to find out who really did it." Could she love him again?

"Because you didn't do this. I couldn't stand by and just let it happen. It's wrong, and it's my fault. They were after me, not you." She moved back, giving him room to get out.

Samantha stuck her head out of the door. "Are y'all coming? They're downloading the recordings."

When they finally walked in, the sheriff was on the phone. Two suits were at the computer. James came over and shook his hand. "There's been developments in the case."

His nerves knotted. Developments were never good when it came to him.

Danica stepped forward. "That was fast."

"It seems the stash found in your Jeep was connected to another case that is connected to Stephanie. A couple of people also called the sheriff's office today." He looked at Danica. "They didn't realize it until later, but they captured some photos with Stephanie around your car. One actually has her opening the back and putting a bag in it." He gave Reid a lopsided grin. "Seems everyone wants to make sure we know you're innocent, even though you confessed." He slapped Reid on the shoulder.

"So, you know he didn't do it?" Her gaze darted to her father, then back to James. "Once she's seen stealing the drugs, he'll be cleared, and everything will be dropped, right?"

"Basically, yeah."

"We got her," one of the suits called out. "We have to take this computer as evidence."

The sheriff joined them. "We have a warrant for her home and office already."

James reached over to place a hand on Danica's shoulder. "Sorry about Steph. I know you counted her as a friend. I didn't see this one coming, either. It's been a crazy day. Why don't y'all clear out and go home? Bobby's here. We'll make sure everything is locked up."

"Good idea." Mr. Bergmann pulled Danica into a hug before turning to leave.

Reid's feet didn't move. He was missing something. "It's over? I can go?"

"You're no longer a suspect. You're still on probation, so don't go all crazy on me, but yes, go home. Get back to work." He left to join the other officers.

Adrian slapped him on the back. "Congratulations. Seems kind of anticlimactic, but that's for the best."

Reid couldn't clear his head. Danica grabbed his arm and pulled him outside. He felt stuck in slow motion. They all climbed back into the Suburban like it was the end of a regular day on the ranch. He wasn't going to prison. He was still free.

The Bergmann sisters started talking at once again as they drove away. Mr. Bergmann eventually pulled into the drive of the family home. The family poured out of the Suburban, everyone except Danica. "Daddy, I'll take Reid home." She crawled out of the back seat. "Reid. You stay right there. I'm going to check on the girls, then I'll be back."

So, he wasn't invited inside. Mr. Bergmann didn't move from his seat, but Reid couldn't take his eyes off Danica as she walked away. The way she moved in the faint light of the early morning seared into his brain. The days were closing in on him. Soon, he would be back to only having memories of her.

At the side door, Danica stopped and looked back at the car. Was she going to invite him in to see the girls? He stopped breathing. His hand on the door handle, ready to open it with one word from her.

She started back to them. "Daddy? What are you doing?"

"You go on. Get inside. It's time Reid and I had a talk." He had rolled down his window.

"Daddy?" There was a warning at the edge of her voice.

"Go on in, Danica."

Reid wasn't sure he wanted a heart-to-heart with Danica's father, but he was right. It was past time.

Standing with hands on her hips, she looked like a warrior. With a shake of her head, she turned and disappeared inside the house.

"Everything worked out tonight, but it doesn't erase the last six years. What exactly are your plans?" The older man kept a tight grip on the steering wheel. His hard jaw popped as if each word he spoke painfully slipped through.

"First, you have to know I'm not the man I used to be. I think Danica saw the potential all those years ago, but I let her down." He took a deep breath. *Lord, give me the words.* "I know it sounds cheesy, but in some ways, prison was the best thing that ever happened to me. Through Ray and his ministry, I truly found the Lord."

"So, Danica should forget and forgive. You want her to take you back?"

Acid burned his gut. "No. But I did want to tell her face-to-face that I was wrong. I hadn't planned on working for her. I had no idea we had children. That sort of changed things for me. I know I don't deserve it, but I want to be their father, even if she no longer wants to be my wife."

With a nod, Mr. Bergmann finally turned to him. Eyes that looked so much like Danica's glared at him. "I haven't always been the best father, but I love my daughters. Anyone that hurts them is not welcome in my home."

"Yes, sir. I—"

"I'm not finished. Six years ago, she brought you home. I basically shut you out for no other reason than I didn't like your background."

"I under—" A sharp glare told Reid to stop talking.

"I was wrong then. I've prayed a great deal about my role as a father this last year. If I had been… I don't know, more open, it would have allowed both of you to talk to me. Better decisions could have been made. All I'm saying now is that I am here for my daughter. If she wants a divorce, then I will help her with that. If she wants you in her life, I will be here to support her and my granddaughters. If you stay, I do pray you are the man of God you claim to be. Their welfare is the most important thing to me. I will always be close. Do you understand?"

"Yes, sir."

"Now, what are your plans with my daughter and granddaughters?"

"I love them. I want a second chance, but that depends on Danica."

Thunder rumbled over the hills, and Mr. Bergmann looked out the open window. "Looks like we might get a morning storm. Those are rare."

Reid frowned. Was there a hidden message, or were they finished? Texans loved talking weather when they had nothing else to say.

Danica darted out of the house and approached, opening the driver's door. "Everything good?"

They both nodded but didn't say anything.

"Okay." She grinned. "Were any real words spoken, or was it just glares and grunts? Seems to be a language you both know."

Her father slipped out of the car and kissed her forehead. "Don't be such a smart-mouth."

She patted his cheek. "Better than being a dumb one. Since I seem to be without a car for now, can we take the green monster?"

"She's all yours." With a nod to Reid, he turned and left.

As the soft rain started tapping the top of the car, Danica climbed in and backed down the long drive. On the road, she glanced at him. "So, what did y'all talk about?"

He shrugged. "Daughters."

"Again?" She laughed. "That must be a loaded topic."

He sat back and enjoyed the sound of her joy. He closed his eyes, trying to memorize it for the days ahead. They settled into silence as the wipers created a rhythm with the rain that fell harder. They needed to talk about the future. He couldn't hang on the edge, not knowing, any longer.

"Reid."

"Danica."

Speaking at the same time, they now slipped back into silence.

He rubbed his forehead. "Sorry. You first."

"I was just going to thank you. You shouldn't have said anything. They didn't even consider you."

"The thought of handcuffs on your skin or the girls seeing you being arrested was... I couldn't let that happen." He shoved his hands in the pockets of his denim jacket. Anything to stop from reaching for her. The need to touch her consumed him at times.

"Danica, I need you to make a decision about my role in the girls' lives. I don't think we can keep it from them much longer."

"I know. But I'm... There has been so much..."

He wanted to drop to his knees and beg her to let him stay, but this needed to be her decision. Calming his nerves, he gripped the Bible tucked into the inside of his jacket.

He took it out and opened the small book, pulling at the faded yellow ribbons. "I can't live on the edge anymore." He laid the strips of cloth on the console between them. "I told you about the song 'Tie a Yellow Ribbon Around the Old Oak Tree,' remember?"

"I do."

"I understand if you don't want me to be part of your life. The girls are thriving without me as their father." Fear of rejection was just his pride talking, not God. He had to put it aside. "I want you to know that I'll always love you. Doesn't matter if I'm in Clear Water or on the other side of the world, my heart will always be with you." Looking down, he ran his thumb over the worn silk ribbons. "I've written my number on these, so if the girls ever want to call me, I'll be there for them."

He swallowed back the acid that burned in the pit of his belly. "I need to know if I'm welcomed, so tie one to the gate if I can come home to you. If I don't see one, I'll keep driving." He kept his gaze down, not wanting to see her reaction. "No awkward goodbye."

"What if I need that awkward goodbye?"

"You mean for closure?" He was sick to his stomach. "Just call me anytime. I'll meet you wherever you want."

Silence filled the space. He wanted to press her, to hear her say she didn't need the ribbons. That he was welcomed. But she stared down the road, and he didn't ask.

Driving through the ranch, she stopped in front of his little bunkhouse. His roommates were sitting on the porch, watching the rain and drinking coffee. They stood and waved, stupid grins stretched across their faces.

"They actually look happy to see me."

"Why wouldn't they?"

He looked at her. "Most people don't like having a housemate that just got out of prison."

"I've found that cowboys for the most part are a pretty loyal group. Once they count you as a friend nothing is going to change that. Plus, they know you didn't steal the drugs from the sanctuary. The foreman even offered to help. He told me to make sure you got back to work as soon as possible."

He looked out the window at Philip and Wade. "They're smiling like idiots."

"They probably know we're married. I'm not keeping it a secret any longer."

His focus jerked back to her. "Everyone knows? Not just your family? What if we get divorced?"

"Then we get divorced. I'm done with secrets." She shrugged as if holding his whole world in her hands was no big deal. To be fair, she didn't know he was giving her full control. He wanted her to come to him because she wanted to, not out of guilt or obligation.

Reluctantly, he went for the door handle. Words swirled in his brain, but he didn't know which ones to use, or how to put them together.

He wanted to be her hero. But he was a McAllister. Not hero material. "I better be going. The sun will be up soon, and we need to be out feeding."

He wanted to hit his head against the window. He was so lame.

"You need to get some sleep."

He grinned. "Don't think a night in jail is a good excuse to miss work."

"You're too hard on yourself." She glanced at the ribbons in her hand as if they held some great knowledge. Looking up, her eyes pulled him back from the opened door.

He had to say something, or he'd regret it

forever. "I'll never be the man you deserve, but no one will ever love you more than I do. No matter what you decide, you will always have my heart."

Without waiting, he turned and launched himself out of the Suburban. In a couple of long strides, he was on the porch. He didn't look back until he heard the big green monster crush the gravel under its tires. Once it was safe, he turned to watch his Dani girl leave.

She paused at the first gate. His phone vibrated.

"Oh, he's already getting a honey-do list." Philip and Wade laughed like they had made the funniest joke, instead of some old lame one.

Thinking the text was from his parole officer, he looked down. It was from her.

His gaze darted to the back of her car. The brake lights turned off, and she vanished into the early-morning rain.

His heart raced as he touched her name.

Her text read, Read Jeremiah 31:3 out loud three times. He frowned and pulled out the Bible tucked in his jacket.

"So, are we going to be breaking in a new wrangler, or is everything good?"

Unable to really focus on Wade's voice, he shook his head to process what they had asked him.

"I think he needs coffee." Philip smirked.

He wanted privacy to read the passage she'd sent him. "It's all good. They found the person responsible." He didn't want to be standing here, talking about nothing. "I'm going to get some coffee."

They both laughed. He didn't care. As soon as he stepped into the small living space, he opened his Bible to Jeremiah. "'Yes, I have loved you with an everlasting love. Therefore, with loving kindness, I have drawn you.'"

He read it out loud again. With one hand, he poured a cup of coffee. Spilling some, he brought his hand to his mouth and licked it off. Sipping the black liquid, he read the verse again.

Something shifted inside him as he repeated the words. God made him and loved him with an everlasting love. He sat in a chair at the old table. No matter what, God loved him.

Despite what his father or mother had done, even despite what he'd done, God wanted him in all his wretchedness and sin. Vile and disgusting, he still had a Father who was willing to wash the filth off him with His own two hands. Reid was only lost, not forgotten. He buried his face in his hands. He fought back the emotions that overwhelmed his body, but he knew without a doubt that God loved him.

Later today, he would find out once and for all if he still had Danica's love, as well.

Danica picked up one of the ribbons and rubbed her thumb over it. At their daughters' age, Reid had already been left alone in the world.

He didn't know it, but what he was asking for was a family. A home to call his own. A place to belong.

Tears fell. She needed to make a decision, and she might not be able to trust her heart.

Dear God, I love him so much. I want to give him that home and family. But is this Your plan for me? Has it always been Your plan for us, or am I trying to control things again?

Sitting in the driveway, she pressed her head against the steering wheel and prayed. The screen door opened and Jackie stepped out into the rain. Nikki followed her. Her twin walked to the car with a pink-and-white umbrella. Nikki just pulled her jacket over her head and ran for the Suburban. The wind pushed rain in when they climbed into the back seat.

Jackie shook out the umbrella and tucked

it under her feet. "I can't believe you chose today to sit out in the car."

"Um… I didn't ask you to join me, and I thought you would both have gone to your own homes by now."

"After everything that happened today? You're joking, right?" Jackie, her straightforward no-emotions-needed sister, had tears in her eyes. "You're married, and you never said anything." She blinked and bit her lips, as if that would stop any unpleasant reaction. "I thought we told each other everything."

All the sisters went quiet, one of the few times in their lives when they had nothing immediate to say.

"I'm sorry." Danica reached out and took her sister's hand. "I was so embarrassed. It was impulsive. When we went back to school, I was so mad at everyone for not giving Reid a chance, then I thought I'd find a way to tell you over the summer. But… well, you know what happened next. He disappeared on me. I was humiliated and ashamed. Instead of trusting you or God, I hid."

Nikki leaned forward. "I wish I had been here for you. Maybe if I had been honest about my pregnancy, instead of hiding, you would have felt safe enough to tell us everything."

Jackie put her hand on top of Danica's and Nikki's. "No more secrets. Agreed? We are a solid wall of love."

"Agreed," they all said in unison.

The screen door opened and Sammi stuck her head out.

Jackie sighed. "Looks like little sister found us."

"Were we hiding from her?" Nikki opened her door and waved her over.

"No, I just think of her as the little sister. We really need to start inviting her to these meetings."

Climbing into the front seat, Sammi shook the water off. "I've given up waiting for an invitation." Her tone brisk, she looked at her older sisters. "So, have we decided what Danica is going to do about her husband?"

Jackie and Nikki giggled like girls. Then Nikki rubbed Sammi's arm. "First, we're glad you joined us. Second, that's what we're trying to find out."

They all looked at her. Her sisters. Her best friends.

She shrugged. "I don't know. I loved him so much, but that doesn't mean Reid should be in my life. Six years ago, one impulsive act set all this in motion. I don't know if I can trust my own judgment."

Nikki sat back. "I can understand that. I was so afraid of my love for Adrian, I almost lost him."

Jackie grunted, sounding just like their dad. The other sisters grinned as they looked at each other. "What?"

"You sound just like dad when he doesn't want to talk about something." Danica winked at her.

Sammi nodded. "Yeah. Like Sonia. I know they're dating, but he won't admit it."

Jackie threw a hand in the air. "Don't get me started on that relationship." She sighed. "But going back to Nikki and Adrian. You can't compare the two men. Adrian was born with an oversize dose of responsibility. He's a solid guy that would never run. Reid is more like Nikki. Adrian loved her, despite her being a flight risk."

"Thanks." Nikki glared.

"Well, it's true. I'm just saying, people can change. A flight risk can settle down." She smiled at Nikki.

Sammi nodded. "Reid has worked so hard since he's been here. I like him. Plus, if you have a parent who wants to be part of their children's lives, you should let them. It's the right thing to do."

Danica's heart broke a little for her baby sister. Her mother had left before Sammi even started school. Then she would return for short periods, playing hide-and-seek in her only child's life. Most of the time it was hiding. "You're right."

"You love him?" Sammi whispered the words.

"Yes. It's hard to believe, but I do now more than I did six years ago."

Nikki leaned closer and reached for her hand. "He seems to love you."

"He says he does." She picked up the ribbons and told them the story of him waiting for his own father to come get him. "Tonight, he said he would stay away if that's what I wanted." She bit her bottom lip to regain some sort of control. "Then he told me his heart would always be mine. No matter what happened between us, he would always love me."

Tears spilled over. She loved him so much, and no one else made her feel as loved as he did.

Jackie put her hand over Danica's. "Do you have any doubt where you belong?"

She shook her head.

Sammi's hand went over Jackie's. "So, you already know what you want."

Nikki joined in. "How can we help?"

Chapter Fifteen

The old ranch truck moved about ten miles under the speed limit as Reid hugged the edge of the curves, driving up and down the hills. The hills that he hoped took him home. Had he made a mistake giving Danica the ultimatum? Tapping the brakes, he slowed the truck again and pulled to the uneven shoulder.

The Bible Ray had given him in prison lay on the empty seat next to him. He wrapped his fingers around the warm leather.

"God, we know I'm not worthy of her, but I can't imagine a life without her. Please hold me as I drive past her place. Let me honor my promise to her to keep going if that's what she wants."

Fear made him sick to his stomach. He promised her that he'd keep driving if she didn't want him. He'd never call or visit again. He'd make it as if he'd never existed if that was what she thought she and the girls needed.

Now, as he sat on the side of the road, he had to find the strength to walk away from the only life he'd dreamed of since meeting her.

The hope of Danica would be lost to him forever. To never see her or his daughters again, to not exist in their world, it would be the most painful life.

Cold sweat sent chills along his neck and down his spine. The sun sat right on top of the hills and slowly climbed into the sky. He lowered his head and prayed. He prayed with every ounce of his being. If he could have laid out flat on the road and turned everything over to God, he would have.

He'd stalled long enough. It was time to rip the bandage from the wound.

Hand over hand, he turned the truck back onto the old ranch road. A big green Suburban came at him. The driver honked, and an SUV full of females waved. It was the Bergmann clan. He glanced at the rearview mirror once they passed. Had Danica been in there? Where were his twins?

Was that his answer from Danica? He swallowed. Had they taken her away in case he didn't keep driving? Taken her away from him?

His knuckles turned white, strangling the steering wheel. But when he saw the first yellow ribbon, his boot slipped off the gas. Pressure built in his chest. A few posts down, another yellow ribbon was tangled in the barbed wire, fluttering in the breeze left behind by the storm.

The big heavy tires dropped another ten

miles per hour. Crawling along the road to the sanctuary's entryway, Reid stared down the long line of cedar fencing. Yellow bows were wrapped around each rough gray post in the sunshine. At the stone-and-iron gate, huge yellow streamers intertwined with the arch of letters that spelled out the original ranch name.

He stopped the beat-up, worn-out truck as the dented grill crossed the cattle guard. The scene in front of him became watery as his eyes stung. She wanted him. She wanted them to be a family.

Voices from the past, his father, his brothers, his prison guards, commanded him to leave. They told him he wasn't good enough. He wasn't made for this life. He didn't have the right to be part of a good family. He would never be the man they needed.

Heavy chains encased his rib cage, pulling tighter until his breath gave up the fight to get to the surface. He inched down the drive. God's voice was stronger than all the other voices combined.

He passed the old bunkhouse where he had first seen her. Where the baby bats slept.

The yellow ribbons led him down a path to the old ranch house he'd helped restore. His dream stood on the porch. His vision blurred. Blinking, he needed to make sure what he saw was real.

Danica's hair was pulled back in a yellow headband. Her curls brushed her bare shoulders. The yellow sundress fluttered at her knees.

The twins jumped in place and waved. Smiling at him, as if excited he had arrived from a long journey home. Wide yellow sashes were boldly tied around their middles over soft purple dresses.

The pressure from the chains pulled tighter. Reid's hand went to the gears, and he put the truck in Park. Ice crawled along his veins, freezing his muscles. Was he dreaming? Danica turned to the girls and spoke with them. His gaze stayed glued to her as she slowly moved down the steps and started walking toward him. Was it a trick? Was she still mad at him, and this was her revenge?

"Reid?" She paused halfway down the drive. "Are you okay?"

Cutting the engine, he sat in complete silence. The voices from his past faded. He took one deep breath and tore away the chains that held him in place. God was on his side and would not allow his past to hold him prisoner any longer. Opening the truck door, he watched as she took another step toward him.

Each step that brought her closer was cautious. She tilted her head. "Reid?"

His gut tightened. Was she really trusting him with her heart? With their daughters?

Boots to the ground, he stood next to the truck. The giant pecan tree that shaded the house was covered with long yellow ribbons dancing in the breeze. Even the porch was covered in yellow. Then he realized he'd painted her home a soft yellow with white trim. He had been asking her to invite him in from the very beginning.

She stood halfway down the drive, concern in her eyes. A golden-red curl crossed her face. With a graceful movement, her long fingers pushed it back, getting it under control.

He took a deep breath. "Are you sure?"

He moved one foot forward, then the ice returned. If she changed her mind, he'd shatter. "Danica, if I go up those steps and walk over that threshold, there will be no going back. I'm never leaving."

A soft smile and a gentle love filled her face. "I'm counting on that."

The last of the chains shattered. He charged forward until she was in his arms. He lifted her up, loving the feel of her as she wrapped her arms around him. She fit against him in the most perfect way. "I'm staying with you forever until God takes me away." Her hands moved up his arms to his face. Soft hands cupped his rough jawline. Now he wished he had taken the time to clean up. "I'm sorry. I should have shaved before I came over."

Leaning closer, she looked straight into his eyes. "You're perfect the way you are." Her lashes lowered, and she pressed her lips against his.

His body melted into her warmth. He was hers. He had always been hers, but now she claimed him. Setting her down and cupping her hands, he pulled back an inch. "I never imagined someone like you could love me."

"Momma!"

"Can we come off the porch now?"

He stepped back. "Do they know?"

She grinned at him. "Maybe. I asked if they thought you'd be a good father for them."

His heart launched out of his rib cage. Swallowing it back down, he glanced over her shoulder to the porch. "What did they say?" The gravel in his throat made it hard to get the words out.

She laughed. "They said they'd been praying that you'd be their father." She took his hand and pulled him toward their girls. "Come on. Let's introduce you to your daughters."

His fingers squeezed hers. His boots hit the steps with a solid thump. They rushed him, their small bodies almost knocking him backward.

Love was a powerful thing. Tangible in his arms. *Thank You, God.*

He closed his eyes and used all his senses to absorb this perfect moment. Danica's hand pressed against his back. The girls' arms tightened around him as they hugged him close.

He was home.

Epilogue

Reid stood on the top step of the restored ranch house. It was finally happening. The old pecan tree shaded the guests sitting on the front yard. The sun was shining, and the air was crisp. A perfect February day in Texas.

Hanging from the tree, long yellow-and-white ribbons danced in the wind with tiny paper hearts tied to the ends. Large white spheres that radiated with light were scattered among the hearts and lined the porch.

They were all waiting. Over three hundred people stared at him, but he didn't notice.

Pastor Levi leaned over. "You need to breathe. You don't want to steal her moment by passing out. I've seen it happen."

As best man, Adrian was on his left. "They aren't even late yet. So, relax. I guarantee you, they aren't letting you get away this time."

On the lower steps, Bobby and Philip chuckled. Reid pulled at his collar. He had never worn a tie in his life.

Derrick, one of the teens from church, sat on the far end of the porch and strummed on a guitar. Then the music changed. Lifting his head, Reid stopped breathing.

They were here. A small herd of women gathered at the new archway that stood at the front of the yard. Samantha opened the wooden gate and marched toward them with the biggest grin on her face. For the first time since he'd known her, she was wearing a dress. They'd joked with her about being one of the groomsmen instead just so she could wear jeans. She did win the battle over shoes, proudly striding forward in her cowboy boots. As she moved to the side, she winked at him. Next was Nikki, followed by Jackie.

His daughters danced through the gate next, waving to people as they threw yellow petals on the ground. When they saw him, they yelled and ran to him. Going down, he opened his arms and pulled them close.

Jackie tried to get their attention. There was some soft laughter from the yard. He was sure they'd broken protocol. But he didn't care. Today, they would become an official family in front of God, the Bergmanns and the whole community of Clear Water.

"We're all getting married today, Daddy."

"Do you like our dresses? Momma said they were a birthday surprise."

"You're beautiful." To be honest, if asked, he probably couldn't tell anyone what they were wearing, but it didn't matter. His daughters loved him.

Little white flowers were pinned in their red curls. "Happy Birthday," he whispered as he kissed each of them on their forehead before sending them over to their aunts.

He couldn't imagine a better way to celebrate this day than showing them how much he loved their mother. The music changed again. Under the wooden arch, standing on this side of the gate, was his bride. His. Bride.

The world disappeared and he lost contact with his own body. Danica was stunning. Tall and elegant, she seemed to be floating toward him. Her hair was pulled up with those same little white flowers, and a yellow ribbon. Long curls fell down her graceful neck.

The February breeze played with her hair. She looked straight at him. A secret smile curved her lips. She was his. And in front of all these people, he would get to stand next to her in holy union. This amazing woman was his. Even more stunning? He was hers.

He clenched his fists and took a deep breath. His dream was within reach. If he went down the two steps, he could hold her and make sure this was real, but he waited. She finally reached him and stopped.

"Who gives this woman to this man?"

"I do, her father. And in memory of her mother." *Aww*'s could be heard throughout the yard.

"Us too! Us too!" The twins jumped up and down, causing light laughter. The last of their flowers were scattered.

This was happening. He glanced at Mr. Bergmann. The older man nodded and laid Danica's hand in Reid's palm, stepping back.

Jackie moved forward to take the bouquet. She narrowed her eyes at him. "Cowboy, don't embarrass yourself in front of the whole town." Her voice was hoarse like she'd been crying.

Oh, man, his eyes were leaking. He gritted his teeth and took Danica's hands in both of his. She anchored him. He focused on their point of contact. Her hands were so much smaller than his, but they were strong hands, graceful and pale with light freckles scattered over her skin.

Pastor Levi cleared his throat. "We have gathered here today to celebrate and renew the vows of a marriage that took place six years ago. Today, before God and family, Reid McAllister and Danica Bergmann McAllister…"

McAllister. Danica had taken his name. He didn't hear anything else the pastor said. At that moment, his world was made up of one woman. His bride. His wife. The mother of his children. His Dani girl.

God had given him gifts greater than anything he could have ever imagined for himself.

Adrian nudged him, and he realized they were exchanging rings. His hand shook as he slipped the simple gold band on her finger. She recited her vows and placed a ring on his.

Claiming him in front of the respectable people of Clear Water, and God.

"You may now—"

Just like his daughters, he couldn't hold back any longer, he needed her in his arms. He grabbed Danica, lifting her off the ground.

Before the pastor could get the whole sentence out, he was kissing her. Laughing, she threw her arms around him and kissed him back.

The girls joined them, hugging their legs. He picked Lizzy up and settled her on his left hip, gripping Danica's hand in his right one. Suzie held her mother's hand as they walked back to the archway as a family. His family.

Lizzy kissed him on the cheek, her arms around his neck. "This is the best birthday party ever!"

He had to laugh, then saw years of extravagant birthday parties ahead of them. Danica leaned in closer to him. "We might have set the expectations a little too high."

He didn't care. Whatever kept his girls happy.

"Happy Valentine's Day to my one true love," she said. "You've always had my heart. I'm so glad you brought it home."

"You are my home, Dani girl. My bride, Mrs. McAllister. My name never sounded so good."

Home. She was his home. A special place God had made just for him.

The twins ran ahead to join the bridal party.

The yellow ribbons danced around them. He leaned in close to her ear. "You are my heartbeat, baby. Never forget that."

Her fingers cupped her jaw. "I never did, Reid." With a soft touch of her lips to his, she whispered, "Welcome home, love. Welcome home."

* * * * *

If you enjoyed THE TEXAN'S TWINS,
look for the first book in the
LONE STAR LEGACY *series,*
TEXAS DADDY.

Dear Reader,

Thank you so much for riding along on my sixth trip to Clear Water, Texas. It might be a fictional town, but it's very much rooted in the real Texas Hill Country and planted deeply in my heart. If you have ever been to Leakey and Boerne, you might see familiar sights.

I hope you enjoyed hanging out with the Bergmann sisters. You can find Nikki's story in *Texas Daddy*. I've had fun getting to know them. Since I have two sisters and several aunts myself, I have found it interesting exploring sister relationships.

Walking with Reid and Danica on this journey was at times painful, but I loved watching their faith and love grow and overcome the hurt and self-doubt from the past. Hope you enjoyed reading their story.

The setting for this story was inspired by pictures of baby bats that Teri Wilson shared with me. It was fun getting to research our local wildlife rescue programs.

Blessings,
Jolene Navarro